VIGILANTE ANGELS

Book II: The Cop

Billy DeCarlo

Wild Lake Press, Inc.

Wilmington, DE

Billy DeCarlo/Wild Lake Press, Inc
P.O. Box 7045
Hackettstown, NJ 07840
billydecarlo.com (blog, newsletter signup)

Publisher's Note: This is a work of fiction. Names, characters, places, and incidents are a product of the author's imagination. Locales and public names are sometimes used for atmospheric purposes. Any resemblance to actual people, living or dead, or to businesses, companies, events, institutions, or locales is completely coincidental.

Cover by Archangel Ink http://archangelink.com/
Editing by WordVagabond https://wordvagabond.com/

Vigilante Angels Book II: The Cop/Billy DeCarlo. -- 1st ed.
ISBN 978-0-9972196-7-8
LCCN: 2017948463

Sign up for the newsletter at billydecarlo.com to stay informed about progress and release dates for new books, audiobooks, and other news.

Previews of upcoming works and short stories by Billy DeCarlo at Patreon.com/billydecarlo.

Other books by Billy DeCarlo:
https://www.billydecarlo.com/index.php/books

To all who have suffered through disease or at the hands of others.

They have sunk deep into corruption, as in the days of Gibeah. God will remember their wickedness and punish them for their sins.

— HOSEA 9:9

Contents

1 CARSON

BRAD CARSON ENJOYED HIS IMAGE in the full-length locker room mirror, adjusting his holster to the angle he preferred—low on his hip like an Old West gunslinger. Despite making detective, he often still preferred his crisply pressed black tactical uniform. He pulled his service semi-automatic from the holster and assumed a firing stance, aiming for his own forehead, then replaced it, laughing.

"It's a good day to bust some bad hombres. You ready to roll, Jackson?" he asked.

"Locked and loaded. Let's hit the Batmobile. I'm in the mood to crack some skulls. Off the record, of course."

The two men left the locker room and walked through the cacophony of the station-house.

"Make way, losers," Carson announced to the room. "Two bad-ass *po*-lice officers coming through. Feel free to admire us, but please don't touch. It's okay to take notes, take pictures. *This* is what you should strive to become."

He paused at a female officer's desk, struck a pose, and said, "Yeah, I'm busy, but try again another time. I'm very booked up. Maybe I'll squeeze you in—or squeeze into you if you catch my drift."

The woman lurched from her chair at him as if to attack, but stopped short.

Carson didn't flinch and laughed at her attempt to faze him.

"Fuck you, Carson," she said.

He moved along and stopped at another desk. "Jesus Christ. Bobby Borata, I do believe you get fatter every time I walk past you. Do you have a desk drawer full of donuts, Bobby?"

A thin wave of laughter wafted through the room, and Carson soaked up the attention. The officer didn't respond, so he tried again. "You've got to shape up, Borata. Square that sloppy uniform away. It looks like you slept in it. Wasn't your old man a Marine? Didn't he teach you anything?"

Bobby looked at him. "Keep my old man out of this, Carson."

"Hard to do, Borata. I'm looking at him hard for this priest murder. Conspiracy and all that. Him and his buddy Moses, who is, shall we say, no longer with us."

"Leave my father alone, Carson," Bobby cautioned again.

"He'll be alone in the joint; except for when he's getting it in the can from his cellmate."

Bobby came out from behind his desk awkwardly and tried to grab Carson, but was expertly placed in a chokehold, his head directed down toward Carson's crotch.

"Do me, Bobby!" Carson yelled as he jerked Bobby's head up and down.

The room erupted in laughter, and a door burst open as Chief of Detectives Patterson emerged. "What the fuck is going on here? Knock this shit off and get your asses to work. Carson, let go of him. *Now*. You're out of line. *Again*. I need to speak to you about it."

Carson released his grip and whispered to Bobby. "You best get back to your martial-arts training, Borata. It'll never top my cage skills, though. If you want to be a cop, get your ass in shape. Get out from behind that desk once in a while." He turned to Patterson. "Sure thing, Chief. I'll pop in as soon as Jackson and I get back from this run. We have a date with a snitch. Can't blow it by being late."

Patterson shook his head. "Don't forget. By the end of your shift."

Carson and Jackson made their way out of the building to their unmarked car in the parking lot. "You drive. I'll ride shotgun today," Carson said.

Jackson started the engine as they strapped in and prepared to leave. "Where to first?" Jackson asked.

"Head on to the 'hood. Back to the Taylor place. I want to shake that nephew down, see if he'll talk to me. Maybe he's ready to say what he knows about old man Borata's involvement with his uncle when he killed the priest."

"You want me to plant a bag on him?" Jackson asked. "That'll give you some leverage."

"Yeah, in fact, that might work. I have to get this investigation moving if I'm gonna get promoted next cycle."

Jackson slowed down as they drove through the city's blighted section. They both lowered their windows and stared menacingly at the people on the street, who froze in place at the sight of them. Movement and conversations stopped until they had moved past. "I love this shit," Carson said. "I love to intimidate. Call me The Intimidator. That'll be my superhero name."

They pulled up next to a strapping, overly-made up woman with a large afro, wearing a short dress standing at a corner. "Hello, honey," Carson greeted her. "Haven't seen you in town before. Got stuck working the early shift today, huh?"

She looked around uncomfortably—as if searching for an escape route.

"Don't be nervous," Carson added. "You know your boss, Charlie the pimp? Well, we're kind of *his* boss. So it's all cool. Except we might need some favors occasionally from you, understand?"

She nodded, and they moved on.

"I believe I'll get me some of that black sugar," Carson said.

"You do know that was a dude, right, Carson?" Jackson asked.

"The hell it was," Carson replied. His face reddened with embarrassment. "These street women are rough, that's all."

"Nah, that was a dude. You just hit on a dude. Maybe you have some latent homosexual tendencies there, Carson."

Carson flew into a rage. "Shut the fuck up, Jackson. Of course I knew it. I was just fucking around, you understand? Nothing more. Don't think about embarrassing me with any shit like that around the station, you understand?"

"Alright, alright. Calm down. Jesus."

Carson continued to fume as they approached a bodega. A large man was leaning against the building, smoking a cigarette. "Hold on, Jackson," Carson said.

They stopped, and Carson got out of the car and approached the man. "What's up, brother-man? You causing trouble?" he asked.

The man looked at him uneasily. "I'm not doing anything wrong. Not holding, not soliciting. Just got off my shift. Graveyard."

"You're loitering though, right? Stay where you are," Carson ordered. He opened the door to the store and summoned the clerk. The Asian woman came outside.

"Didn't you call in about some guy shoplifting?" Carson asked her.

"Wait a minute, what is this?" the man objected.

"Shut up, or you're going down," Carson responded sharply.

The clerk looked confused, appearing to wonder if she'd heard him correctly. "No. Nobody cause trouble today. Quiet day so far."

"Go back inside," Carson ordered her. She eagerly complied.

Jackson got out of the vehicle and walked over. "Is this man resisting arrest, Detective Carson?" he asked.

"He might be in a minute. Let's see." Carson grabbed the man and spun him, pushing him up against the wall.

"Come on, I ain't doing nothin'," the man complained.

Carson kicked his legs apart and yanked his hands behind him, cuffing them tightly. He jammed his elbow into the center of the man's back and pushed his face into the wall. "Hold still," he shouted. Carson turned to enjoy the attention from the passing traffic as cars slowed to watch what was happening. He patted the man down, yanking bills, change, cigarettes, and a lighter out and onto the sidewalk.

Jackson picked up the pack of cigarettes and ripped the top open, dumping them onto the street. He examined them to see if any were joints. "All clear," he said.

Carson removed the cuffs and spun the man back around. His face was bleeding, and he wore an angry scowl.

"Police brutality. You should be ashamed of yourselves," he said.

Carson laughed as they got back into their car. "Have a nice day, buddy. Stay outta trouble." He picked up a few of the larger bills. "And thanks for the tip." As they pulled away, he watched the man bend to pick up his belongings. "I love this job."

"We're just keeping the streets safe for the citizens, in our own special way," Jackson added. "You know, too bad he was clean. The more of them we put into cages, the cleaner and safer my city becomes."

"We need a bigger zoo," Carson laughed. "There they are, just up ahead, dancing in the street like a bunch of goddamn monkeys. Hold up here and let's watch for a few minutes. Maybe they'll fire up a joint. Then park as close to those bikes as you can, block them in. Call our location in to the station while we wait."

2 ROUGH RIDER

LUKAS TAYLOR STOOD and stretched, bending backward with his hands on his hips. The early spring sunrise crested the decaying apartment buildings nearby, bathing the group and their motorcycles in warm light. "Damn, it's hard getting anything done with these busted-up old tools and junkyard parts," he complained to the group around him.

"I keep saying it don't pay to be honest," Gary said. "I keep telling you. We ain't getting out of this 'hood working our shit-paying jobs. We got to hustle. We can barely put gas in our tanks, Lukas. I don't want to break bad, my man, but this poverty is gettin' old. After those motherfuckers took the towers down a few years ago, we should've all signed up for the military. We'd be out soon and all set with GI benefits."

Lukas slapped him on the back and gripped his shoulder. "You can't get me down, brother. Sun's shining. Let's finish these repairs and ride."

He reached over to a boom box on the curb, punching a few buttons and turning a knob to bring it to life. "Take a break, Black Eagles," he told them. "Easy old-school ghetto morning music." As the first strains of Marvin Gaye's "Sexual Healing" began, he looked up and pointed one of the two tire irons in his hands at a closed window above. "This one's for you, Uncle Mos. Rest in peace!" he declared.

The other Eagles, five men and a woman, paused to watch as Lukas began a practiced choreography, flipping the steel irons high in the sunlight, twirling them, grabbing them from the air, and relaunching them. He folded his muscular body lower and lower, until he morphed the routine into a break dance, spinning his body on the cardboard sheets they'd laid out on the street for their repairs.

"Go on, kick it, Luke," Tass said above the music. She dismounted her bike, sauntered over to him, and began dancing. Her lithe body moved in sync with Lukas and the music, with just the faintest traces of sweat beginning to show on her tight-fitting ribbed tank top.

The other Eagles rose from their milk crates and bikes and joined in, filling the sidewalk with their writhing bodies, laughing and clapping to the beat. The sun fully revealed itself and bathed them in its glow, erasing the dullness of the surrounding concrete and steel.

As the song wound to its finish, a voice came from a fire escape above. "You all either drunk or crazy. It's too damn early on a Sunday to be acting foolish. People got to rest."

Lukas looked up, smiling. "Aw, come on, Miz' Irving. Take that robe and headscarf off and let your beautiful 'fro fly free. Come on down and dance with the Eagles on this sunny day. Ain't nobody drinking. We're good Eagles, can't drink and fly…" He motioned to the bikes.

"Huh. If you ain't drunk, I'm going with crazy. You all be careful on those damn bikes."

She pulled her bathrobe sash tight and went back into her apartment.

"Uncle Mos would've liked the tribute, Luke," Tass said.

Lukas put the tire irons into a long toolbox and looked back up at the window to his uncle's former apartment. "Yeah. I sure miss him sticking his big-ass head outta that window to lecture us."

"He was the boss," Gary said solemnly. "Boss Mos. Now there's a man who didn't go out quietly. Took his stand and took him out some *evil* when he killed that child-molesting priest. I hope nobody ever rents that place up there again. That man deserves a shrine."

"Yeah," Lukas replied. "Remember him and that crazy white man Tommy? Couple of old cancer vigilantes. If I got the big C, I think I might do the same. Why not?" He paused to reflect. "Remember the first day Tommy came around, driving that big-ass Buick?"

A few of them laughed at the thought. "I heard on the news that the cops are talking to him about how the priest died, asking if he had anything to do with helping Moses," Tass said.

"They won't find anything," Lukas answered. "Uncle Mos did what he did on his own. He left that letter explaining it, and that's that." He spoke with a tone of finality to subtly remind the group that the topic was off-limits. "I saw Tommy a while back," he continued. "He said the cops are still hassling him, though. He's still fighting the cancer—wasn't looking too good at all. Uncle Mos sure loved that sumbitch. Said he brought life back into his life, for a little while anyway."

They sat for a while, catching their breath, enjoying the silence of the morning.

"Uh-oh, five-oh coming down the road," Tass said.

They followed her gaze and watched as an unmarked police cruiser accelerated toward them. It swerved in close to the row of bikes and came to a quick halt.

"Be cool, Eagles," Lukas cautioned.

The passenger door swung open and struck the front wheel of the last bike, causing it to topple over onto the street with a crunch, glass particles from the side mirror spraying out next to it.

Lukas moved toward the emerging cop. "What the fuck, man? That's my ride."

"Sorry, bro. Jackson here just got his license," the officer responded.

Jackson got out of the driver's side. "Is this individual giving you some trouble, Officer Carson?" he asked.

"Could be. You're Taylor, right? Lukas Taylor?" Carson asked.

"I am," Lukas responded. "We ain't doing nothin' wrong here. We don't want any problems."

"Come on over by the car, Taylor. We just need to ask a few questions about an investigation. Private, away from your crew." He took hold of Lukas' elbow and guided him back over to the driver's side of the cruiser. "Officer Jackson, can you just make sure he's not carrying any weapons?"

Gary stepped forward. "Oh, come on man. You got no cause to be thinking that…"

Carson stepped in front of him as Jackson placed Lukas against the cruiser and spread his feet. "Stand down, brother man."

"Let it go, Gary," Tass said. "Let's just get them out of here and get on with our business. You know Luke's clean."

"Oh, really, young lady? What kind of *business* are we talking about? You all dealing from the street out here?" Carson asked her.

"Hell no," Tass answered. "Nobody here even got a record. We got jobs. We're just fixing and cleaning up our bikes."

Carson turned toward Jackson, who was finishing his frisk of Lukas. Jackson pulled a hand out of Lukas' sweatpants and held up a small plastic bag half-filled with white powder.

"Well, well," Carson said. "Sure doesn't look like motorcycle polish to me. More like cocaine."

Lukas looked up at the bag and immediately tried to turn. "Bullshit! You put that shit on me. I don't know nothing about that."

"That's what they all say," Jackson said, slamming him back against the cruiser. He pulled his cuffs as Lukas broke away, shoving him backward. The rest of the Eagles rose up at once toward the two officers.

Carson and Jackson moved in unison, backing off a few steps and pulling their sidearms out, pointing them at the group. "Stand down, that's an order," Carson shouted.

"Stay there," Lukas warned the Eagles. "Nobody's getting shot here today. Don't give them an excuse."

Jackson moved to the vehicle and grabbed the radio, calling for backup.

The standoff continued for a few long, tense minutes as the group engaged in derisive discourse with the officers, who continued to point their guns at them.

"Here comes your ride, Taylor," Carson finally announced, as another police car came toward them from one end of the street and a police van from the other, sirens wailing and lights flashing.

Lukas remained silent as the vehicles rolled to a stop and cut their sirens. More officers got out to cover them. Carson holstered his weapon and approached him, throwing him back against the car and cuffing his hands behind him.

"Don't say nothing, Luke," Tass shouted to him. "Don't say nothing. Get a defender. It's bullshit."

Carson pulled him to the back of the van. Lukas stepped up, watching the rear bumper, then felt a hand on his neck and heard, "Watch your head, buddy," as his forehead was pushed into the top of the van and stars swirled in his vision.

He was tempted to complain, but kept his dignity, not giving Carson the pleasure. He knew it would be futile. Carson followed behind him, shoved him down onto the bench seats, and pulled the doors closed behind them.

"Stop resisting, Taylor," Carson yelled for the benefit of the others outside, slamming his forearm into Lukas' face.

"You need help in there?" Jackson called to him.

"Nope, just strapping him in." Carson reached behind Lukas' hips and pulled the seat belts around either side of him, placing them in his lap as if they were connected.

"They're not buckled," Lukas said as Carson opened the doors and exited the van.

Carson winked at him. "Yeah, I know. Have a nice trip," he said as he slammed the doors shut to secure the van.

Lukas began to call out to let his friends know, but felt the words bounce back at him from the reinforced sides of the police van. He wanted to pound on the walls but figured that would only add to their argument that he was being disorderly, and the cop would beat him further. Before he had time to think, he heard the front door open and then slam shut, and saw Carson and Jackson up front, looking at him through the small partition. Carson was behind the wheel.

He felt the van moving slowly down the street. As they took the first turn, his body was thrown across the small space, crunching against the other side of the van and sliding down to the floor.

He tasted the blood that filled his mouth and felt it flowing on his head and face as he was tossed from one side of the van to the other. The vehicle increased its speed, and Carson took each turn faster than the last. Lukas heard laughter from up front. It felt as if his arms were being pulled from their sockets each time he rolled across the floor.

In his last moments of consciousness, he imagined himself as an empty soda can being thrown around the back of a pickup truck, back and forth.

3 MEDICAL EVENT

TOMMY LEANED BACK on the park bench and let the afternoon sun wash across his face. He welcomed the unusually warm spring weather, but even on better days, he could feel the effects of the experimental drugs he was taking and the chemo treatments he'd been enduring. *Always cold, always weak. But it's nice not to have to worry about skin cancer anymore.*

A group of children playing nearby caught his attention. He found himself enjoying their shrieks as they held on to a spinning roundabout. *Once upon a time, that noise would have driven me nuts.*

As he watched them, he struggled to keep his eyes focused, and he felt dizzy. He thought back to his childhood, remembering himself and his friends enjoying the same playground equipment so many years ago. *It's good that some things don't change. I wish I could go back. Maybe in the afterlife.*

He thought about the brevity of his life, and how it seemed like just a few years ago that he was a boy with grand aspirations and no understanding of how easy it would be to become sidetracked from them. With his recent cancer diagnosis, all he could focus on was the past, and how he had wasted so much of his life. He knew there wasn't going to be much future.

He carried the guilt of his mistakes: the times he was a bad husband and father, his racism, his refusal to acknowledge his son's homosexuality. He granted himself some absolution for making an effort to change in the past year and was more at peace with who he was now.

He counted the things he had to be thankful for: a good wife, a son who loved him despite ample reason not to. He was okay financially, due to his police pension and their frugal lifestyle, and he was still alive beyond the oncologists' initial projections.

He slouched back, and the sun glinted off the gold medallion that hung at his chest. The flash caught him in the eye and disoriented him. He took the pendant in his hand and examined it. *Saint Michael, the archangel, Moses said when he gave it to me. Spiritual warrior who fought evil and protected the innocent. Protector of cops.* He let it fall back to hang on its chain.

He was strangely unsettled, and closed his eyes. Opening them again, he momentarily felt confused. *Fucking cancer meds have me all screwed up. The cure is worse than the disease.*

He attempted to return to watching the children play, and tried to remember why he'd come to the park. He was considering leaving when he saw a familiar figure approach. He struggled for the man's name. *It's like I'm drunk all over again, somehow.*

"Tommy Borata," the man called. "Best cop I ever worked with. How's it hanging? Retirement treating you well?" the man asked, taking a seat next to him.

Tommy stared and struggled until the man's identity finally came to him. "Hey, Chief Patterson. I dunno. I'm all screwed up from all these different types of pills they're giving me. Don't know who I am or where I am sometimes. Like right now."

"Hang in there, buddy. The science is getting better all the time."

"I'm trying. It's a shitty way to live. Almost as bad as when I had to work with you every day. How's your cousin doing, Roger? The one who had the same thing as me."

Patterson took a seat next to him and changed the subject. "Listen, I don't have a lot of time. Got to get back to the office. I got a coupla things I wanted to talk to you about."

"Go ahead. I got terminal cancer, so I ain't got a lot of time either."

"You always did have a sick sense of humor, Borata. It's just this cop, Carson. The one who just made detective and won't let the priest thing go. That asshole's getting out of control. He's picking on your kid a lot. I'm trying to manage it, but I wanted to let you know so you could be there for Bobby. Just be supportive without letting him know I said anything."

"That motherfucker better leave my kid alone," Tommy said, raising his voice. "I'll fucking…"

"Whoa," Patterson cut him off. "Don't be saying anything around me. You know how that shit works. And don't get involved in station politics, please. It puts me in a bad spot. Just take care of your kid. I'll deal with it on the other side. It's complicated. Carson's got some kind of cover way up the chain. Disciplinary actions against him always get overturned somehow."

"You think he's crooked?" Tommy asked.

"Something's going on. It's bigger than me, that's for sure. I'm close to retirement, and I have to pick my battles. All I know is that he's a pain in the ass, and acts like he's invincible as far as any kind of consequences for his behavior. I sent it up to internal affairs, but haven't heard a word. Maybe they're on it, or maybe they're *in* on it. I don't know. I'm just giving you the heads up concerning Bobby, and asking you to leave it alone on the other side."

"What is it these days? Is it me, or has all sense of integrity and morality gone from society? Nobody follows the rules anymore.

Greed seems to be the only thing that matters. There's even more prejudice and racism. It seems like we're going backward instead of forward."

Tommy grabbed the arm of the park bench to steady himself, as if afraid he'd fall off. "I feel bad about all the shit I used to believe—the way I acted to people who looked different from me or talked different from me. Now I dream about what the world would be like if we could all stop hating people who're different, and stop caring so damn much about having so much dough."

"I don't know the answer, Tommy. I see it too. I'm about done working, and I can't wait. Sarah and I are looking forward to a long retirement together down South somewhere."

The words stung Tommy. "Yeah, well, just hope you don't get sick and die right away, like me."

Patterson grabbed him by the shoulder. "Just a setback, old friend. You're as tough as nails. You're gonna be okay. That's an order!

"About Bobby, though. Why don't you talk to him about doing something else? I really don't think he's happy in the job."

Tommy sat back, watching the children play, now remembering Bobby on the same playground as a happy young boy. *I haven't seen him really happy in so long.*

"Your cousin, though, how's she doing?" he asked again.

Patterson paused as if considering whether he should answer. "Listen, Tommy. One other thing. Like I said, Carson still has a bug up his ass about the priest thing. He's still looking into this, digging around. I think he wants some kind of important win to boost his chances for promotion. He's bragging that he's going to break something big very soon. It's probably more of his bullshit.

"I know you got nothing to worry about, but watch yourself, okay? I don't put anything past him, including making up whatever evidence he thinks he needs to nail you on some trumped-up conspiracy or accessory charge. As far as I'm concerned, the case has been resolved."

Tommy felt his stomach sink hard at the reminder of what had happened in the past year. It brought everything back to him: his friendship with Moses, their plans to kill the pedophile priest. Moses' cancer was growing so quickly. How Moses had betrayed Tommy by executing the plan and the priest on his own, and how he'd died in the process.

"Yeah, yeah. Fuck him. I'm dying anyhow. Fuck him. Roger, you didn't tell me about your cousin."

Patterson finally gave in. "She's passed, Tommy. I'm sorry…"

Tommy was silent, absorbing the information, now well aware of his own mortality and how much time he likely had left. Patterson was asking him something about Margie, but the sound was distant and garbled. *Margie? That's my wife, right?*

He tried to speak. "What time's it getting to be? I gotta get outta here." His voice sounded like it was coming from a tape recorder with a dying battery, slow and garbled. He extended his arm to read his wristwatch. As he did, he watched the arm jerk in a spasm. The entire scene before him seemed as if he were looking at it through a tunnel.

"What the fuck was that?" he heard Patterson ask. "You okay, Tommy?"

Tommy started to get up. He fell back onto the bench, and then tried again, supporting himself with the armrest. He stubbornly forced himself up and felt the world begin to darken.

The sounds of the children and sight of them on the roundabout were distorted as he felt himself spinning, disoriented. His vision blacked out and his stomach gave a sickening lurch as he fell. Someone caught him and laid him down on the bench, his limbs thrashing. He heard a voice yelling for an ambulance, and everything faded to black.

4 LOVERS

MARGIE BORATA LAY BACK against her pillow, twisted the cap from a miniature bottle of scotch, and dumped the contents into a paper cup filled with ice and soda. She stared down into it as it bubbled and fizzed. "I think Bobby knows," she finally said.

Jack sat up straight on the bed. "What? You mean he knows about me? Did he tell Tommy? I don't need that crazy fucker showing up at my house with a gun. And your sister would kill us both."

Margie swirled the cup slowly to mix its contents and then took a long drink. "Yes, she would. She called the house the other day. I'd told Bobby I was going to lunch with her, but you and I were here. So that's what made him suspicious.

"It upset me when he told me that, so I didn't ask him any questions. I don't know if he said anything to her, or brought you into it. But he knows I was with someone I wasn't supposed to be. He's a cop too, after all."

"Ah, for chrissakes. I told you not to use that excuse. See, this is what happens when you're drunk. You walked right the fuck into it. Goddamn it, Margie." He got up from the bed, leaving her there alone, and began to dress. "Now I don't know what the fuck I'm coming home to with Diane."

She began to cry and downed the rest of the drink with a rattle of ice. "Well, you said we would tell them, so we could be together. So maybe this is good..."

He checked himself in the bathroom mirror and pulled out a comb to fix his hair. "Fuck that! Look what you just did. That was *maybe someday* we would do that. Not now. Your husband has cancer. What the fuck are we going to do, tell him that you've been fucking your sister's husband while he's dying? I still have a teenager, I'm in debt, my job situation is shaky, and I don't want to pay goddamn alimony and child support. Fuck, Margie!"

She put the empty cup on the nightstand. "So, it was never true then. You were lying, just using me all of that time. I love you, Jack. Don't you love me? You said you did. You said it every time you were fucking me. Come to think of it, that was the only time…"

She continued to cry as she eased herself from the bed and began searching between the sheets for her underwear. She lost her balance and reached out to the mattress for support.

"See, you're drunk, Margie. That's how you make mistakes. You gotta go easy on that shit. C'mon. Calm down, now."

Her sobs increased in volume as she continued dressing. "I'm just going to tell him. I don't know what else to do. You don't love me! You won't say it…"

He moved to her and embraced her. "Okay, okay. Settle down. Let's figure this out. Sit down here on the bed with me. Maybe it's not so bad."

"What do you mean?" she asked, now a bit calmer.

"Well, maybe Bobby doesn't know it's me…"

"So you're only worried about yourself, asshole?" she yelled, starting to get up again.

He pulled her back down and closer to him. "No, stop. Wait. I mean, there's no sense in blowing the lid off this if we don't have to. You don't want to hurt Tommy, do you? How about you just feel Bobby out about it? Maybe he'll back off. Wait a little, alright?"

"And what if he doesn't?"

"Then it's Plan B. Sit down and talk to your son. He's a man. Tell him you were lonely, but it's over and who you were with is unimportant. Tell him that you don't want to hurt his old man, him being sick and all. Let's take it step by step. Hold on, be quiet a minute. I'll call Diane to see what's up there."

He picked up his mobile phone from the dresser, pressed a number on his speed-dial, and waited until his wife answered. "Hi, honey!" he greeted her in a cheerful voice.

Margie frowned and retrieved the cup, draining the melting ice to get the last few drops of scotch. The ice rattled again as she lowered the drink, and Jack glared at her.

He listened to his wife on the other end. "Yeah, yeah, honey. Another tough day at the office. Another day, another dollar, you know? So, do you want me to bring home some Chinese? The usual?"

Margie looked at herself in the mirror across the room as he continued the upbeat conversation. She wondered how she had transformed from an intelligent, attractive high-school graduate full of dreams to the slightly overweight, hopeless, used-up woman she saw sitting on the rumpled motel bed in her bra and panties. She rose and continued to dress.

"Yes, yes! Let's do that this weekend...Alright, honey...yes...that movie sounds great...love you too, lovey-dovey. Love you to pieces. Be home soon, g'bye." He hung up and continued cleaning up in the bathroom. "See? It's all good," he called out to Margie. He dumped the contents of a small bottle of mouthwash into his mouth and gargled loudly.

"You mean, all good for you, *lovey-dovey*!" she said bitterly. "Fuck you, Jack!" She moved around the room hastily, gathering up her belongings as he patted on some cologne.

His silence annoyed her further. "Jack! What about us? Do you love me? Or are you just going to throw me aside and stay with her? You said after Tommy's gone we'll move away somewhere together. You said it, Jack."

He took a moment to respond. "Of course," he said. "Let's cool it a bit, let this blow over. We're going to be okay, Margie. A lot of changes are coming. Let's be patient." He pulled a dollar from his billfold and placed it on the pillow for the maid.

"*Of course* what? Which one? And you still didn't say it. You can't even say it."

"Okay, okay. Of course I'm leaving her. Christ. I love you, Margie. Let's get out of here, it's about quitting time at work, so I gotta go. Let's just see who knows what and take it from there."

They stood at the door, ready to leave, staring at each other. She just shook her head. They performed a quick embrace and peck on the lips and went out of the motel door a few minutes apart, as they always did.

LESIONS

DARKNESS AND SILENCE were the first things Tommy sensed when he regained consciousness. He lay still, unsure where he was. Slowly his mind cleared and his eyes adjusted. He heard the familiar soft, steady beep of medical equipment. In the darkness of the room, he could see the red and green glow of the instruments. He felt his arm for the IV tube he knew would be there.

Closing his eyes, he tried to recall what had happened. After some effort, he remembered being in the park, but that was all he could come up with.

"Hey. How're you doing?"

The voice caused him to jump, and he strained to find its source.

"Easy, Pop. It's me, Bobby. Take it slow."

He looked over and saw the bulk of his son in silhouette, sitting on a chair against the wall. He felt a strange sense of pride that Bobby was there for him at what he guessed was a very late hour. And that he hadn't turned on the TV and wasn't playing a video game. "Hey, kid. How's it going?"

"Better than it is for you, that's for sure."

"What happened? What happened to me? Car accident?"

"You were in the park with Chief Patterson. You had a seizure. It's a good thing he was there; he got you an ambulance quick."

"Seizure? Why?"

"The docs are working on all of that. They'll be in to see you in the morning. They'll figure it out."

Tommy began to recall more of the scene before his incident. *Children playing. Patterson.* He remembered reminiscing about having watched Bobby play happily in that same park. "Hey, Bobby. I was thinking...damn, time goes fast, you know? I made a lot of mistakes. I'm sorry. I knew early—about you, I mean—and I should have accepted you as you were, instead of fighting it, trying to change you…"

Bobby cut him off. "Pop, enough. We can't change the past. Nothing from nothing; you made me tough enough to handle everything that comes with it. It ain't easy being a gay cop."

The early morning light was beginning to seep into the room. Tommy remembered Patterson's warning about what his son was being subjected to at the station. "Yeah, I bet. A lot of assholes in the station. So-called alpha males and alpha females. Most are chicken-shit when you put them in a scary spot. I've seen it time and again. Big talkers. Why don't you get the hell outta there?"

"It's a tough thing to do, Dad. You were a cop. Grandpa was a cop. I always felt kind of obligated. I wanted to make you both proud. But I guess I haven't done much of that by sitting behind a desk."

"You always made me proud, Bobby. Everything you did. I just didn't always let on. Like when you got your black belt at fourteen. That Sensei Molletier was a taskmaster. It's something I never accomplished, but you did. If you want to look for something else, if that makes you happy, please do it. Life's too short to live for other people, or let them live vicariously through you."

"Thanks, Dad. I'll think about it. I've *been* thinking about it. Another thing, I'm gonna move out. I got a place, with a roommate."

"Guy roommate?" Tommy asked.

Bobby shifted uncomfortably. "Uh, yeah."

Tommy momentarily fought his old instincts, his old persona, and then recovered. "That's good, son. I want you to be happy. But consider what we just talked about. Everything eventually makes its way into that squad room. It's going to be a tough place."

"Yeah, I know. I can handle it. But yeah, I'm looking around, too."

They let it go at that, and Tommy drifted back to sleep.

A tap sounded at the door, along with a rustling of papers. It swung open and a physician entered. The sun was now streaming in through partially opened blinds.

"The good Dr. Mason, how are ya?" Tommy asked. "This is my son, Bobby."

"Hello, Bobby." He began examining Tommy. "I'm doing better than you, Borata. What the hell did you get yourself into now?" the doctor asked.

"Jesus," Tommy taunted back. "You're the one supposed to be answering the questions, pal."

"Oh, right. Time to earn the paycheck. I have car payments to make!" He referred to the notes on his clipboard, taking a seat at the foot of Tommy's bed.

"So, Tommy," he began. "What we have here are a few spots on the brain. That's what caused your seizure. We can fix it…"

"The cancer?" Tommy interrupted. "It's in my fucking brain now?"

"Easy, pal. Easy. We did the scans. These are small, and they're situated such that we can zap them. No surgery. We just zap them out. It's not a big deal. After that, we keep an eye on it."

"That sounds okay, Pop," Bobby added. "Could be a lot worse."

"Yeah," Tommy said with obvious dejection. "Another setback, though."

"Listen, Tommy," the doctor said, rubbing his leg through the sheets. "Treating cancer is like crossing a wide river. We always need to find the next rock to step on to help us across. The trials we've had you on have helped a great deal, but sometimes little things like this pop up. It's like whack-a-mole. But we still have ammo in our clip, to use parlance you might be familiar with.

"There's one very promising trial we're looking at if you test positive for the right mutation, so we have a plan. This is a new drug called Forbaxatel; it's been very effective for some patients with your type of cancer. It also seems to rejuvenate some patients. I hesitate to say it, but it's somewhat miraculous, so far. When it works, that is. It's early in the trial process, so we don't know a lot about the long-term effects yet."

"It's pretty fucked up I have to hope for a mutation," Tommy said glumly.

"Good thing you were always a mutant, Dad," Bobby said, laughing.

Tommy added a forced smile, his mind a long way away.

The doctor rose. "Don't feel bad. All cancers are mutations, and we all have them inside of us. So, we're gonna keep you here, eating this delicious food, for a day or so. Just to observe and get these radiation treatments done. Rest, and put some mind-garbage on the TV. I'll be in checking on you from time to time. Keep your hands off my damn nurses, Borata."

The comment finally brought a genuine smile from Tommy. "Okay, Doc. You got it."

The doctor left, and Bobby moved over to take his place at the foot of Tommy's bed. "One more thing, Dad. I stepped out a few minutes ago and heard over the radio that Carson had picked up Moses' nephew Lukas. They found a baggie on him. They were taking him to the station, and I guess his seat belt came off somehow in the wagon. He's here in the hospital—a little busted up, but he'll be okay. I tried to check in on him when I got here, but he was asleep. They have a guard posted."

Tommy's face reddened, and he felt anger surge through his body. "That's all bullshit. He doesn't use. Just weed. You know damn well that had to be a plant by Carson and his asshole partner. And I'm sure the seatbelt thing was no accident, either. Son of a bitch."

Bobby began to gather his things. "Don't let it get to you. You have enough on your plate. I'll check into it. Maybe I can get close to Carson and get something on him. I got a shift to pull, Dad. Get some rest. I'll be back after work. I'm sure Mom will be in to harass you in a little while."

"Okay, kid. Be careful on the job. Stay away from Carson, but don't take any shit from him. Tell that idiot that I said, 'Fuck you.'"

Bobby laughed. "I'll be sure to do that. Love you, Dad," he said, looking back as he reached the door.

"Love you, son. Always loved you."

Tommy watched the door sweep to a silent close.

6 INTERROGATION

LUKAS GROANED AS HE REACHED for a cup of water on the stand next to his hospital bed. The officer tasked with guarding him turned at the sound and watched his effort with amusement. Heavy footsteps sounded in the hall, and the officer turned to have a low conversation with someone out of sight.

A nurse entered and took his vitals. "Do you need anything for pain, Mr. Taylor?" she asked.

Lukas nodded, and she went about preparing the medication.

Moments later Carson came in, smiling. "Mr. Taylor. I cannot express how sorry I am about our faulty equipment. On behalf of the department, I do apologize. Nurse, would you give us a few moments, please?"

She nodded, then finished up and left.

Carson continued. "However, Mr. Taylor, I am still suspicious that you may have been trying to escape from the van, and noted that in my report on the incident."

"Uck you," was all Lukas could muster though his wrapped and damaged jaw. To make his point clear, he raised his uninjured arm and produced a middle finger.

"Oh, now, let's not get testy. After all, you have a pretty serious charge against you. That coke is some bad shit. We've been trying to track down the supply sources into the city. Looks like it might be a certain motorcycle gang you're involved with."

Lukas tried to rise up, but the cop grabbed the front of his gown and forced him back down, pushing his back into the bed. Lukas gasped in pain.

"Listen. Let's make this easy. Give me what you have on the white guy that was running around with your uncle before he killed that priest. You know the guy—Tommy Borata. I know he was involved somehow. You must've heard them discussing it, or maybe your uncle talked to you. That's all I need. Then all this business about resisting arrest, striking an officer, and carrying dope can just go away."

Lukas stared back defiantly, and the cop leaned harder on his chest. He tried not to react, but couldn't withhold a wince.

"What are you doing to him?" a voice from the doorway demanded. Carson turned and stepped away from the bed, allowing Lukas to see a Latina nurse coming at them. She shoved the officer away and moved to check on him.

"He was trying to tell me something," Carson said. "His jaw is all fucked up; I couldn't hear. I was just leaning in closer to try to understand him."

She turned back to him angrily and took note of his name tag. "Yeah, nice try Officer…Carson. His gown is still all bunched up at the neck from where you were grabbing him. Get out of here."

He looked at her name tag in return. "Don't tell me what to do, Nurse Carmen." He looked at Lukas. "Think about what I said, Taylor," he added as he left the room.

"Assho," Lukas said to the nurse, nodding in the direction of the door.

"Yeah, too many of them are, unfortunately," she said. "Hi, Lukas. I'm Carmen, the head nurse in the oncology wing. I think you know Tommy Borata, right?"

Lukas nodded in the affirmative.

She continued to speak while making him comfortable, adjusting his bed and pillows. "He's here too. Had a seizure, but he's going to be okay. He was worried about you—sent his son to ask me to check in. I'm glad he did.

"Anyway, I talked to the doc, nothing's broken. You've got a mild concussion, but we won't need to admit you. He'll be in shortly with instructions. In the meantime, keep the pager button handy and hit it any time they come in. Always make sure a nurse is in here with you."

"Anks," he said.

She turned the television on for him and flipped through channels until he nodded at one showing a baseball game. She made sure his water pitcher was refilled and consulted with the nurse on duty before coming back to sit by his bed.

"Take care of yourself, Lukas." She took his good hand and squeezed it. She left, and Lukas turned his attention to the baseball game.

A while later, he heard a commotion outside of his station. He could see Tass having words with the cop. She shoved him as he laughed at her, and entered the room shaking her head. "Motherfucker has some nerve, calling me 'brown sugar' after the bullshit they pulled on us today. Racist assholes, all of them. How you doin', Luke?"

Lukas formed an okay sign with his thumb and index finger, then motioned toward the door with his middle finger and shook his head.

"I'm getting you outta here soon, and I ain't leaving until then. Pisses me off—people only see black people's reaction to getting treated the way we just did. They never show *why* we're so angry. Countless blacks incarcerated and executed over decades, generations, but let one cop get hurt or killed and the big, bad black people are plastered all over the damn news. What happened to *us* this morning should be on the news."

Lukas took her hand and patted it, trying to calm her. He pulled it to his mouth and gingerly kissed it. That seemed to break her foul mood, and she smiled at him.

"I kind of like this," she said. "I can talk and talk, and you can't say shit."

He issued a fake groan and a faint smile.

"Anyway, I been thinking. Why don't we give it another shot? I miss you, Lukas Taylor. And you ain't shit without me, right?"

He winked at her and nodded in the affirmative.

"Good answer, because you know, in the shape you're in, I could kick your ass right now, buddy." She leaned in and kissed his bruised lips, and he closed his eyes to enjoy it.

"Ove you, 'ass," he tried to say.

"You always did, didn't you? We don't do well apart. I keep dreaming about us getting the hell out of here. Out of the city. We work at the VA; they're all over the country. What the hell we doin' here? Your uncle is gone, and I don't have much family. You want to ride off into the sunset with me, Lukas Taylor?"

"I do," he managed.

"I do?" she asked. "Like in marriage 'I do'? You trying to propose to me, Mr. Lukas?"

"I do," he repeated.

"Yes!" she shouted, leaning in again to hug him. Lukas groaned and smiled.

7 VISITORS

TOMMY DIVERTED HIS ATTENTION from the window as the door to his room opened. "Nurse Carmen! What a sight for sore eyes. What brings you to the neighborhood?"

"You do. I take care of my patients no matter where they are. How're you feeling?"

"Not bad. Ready to get out of here, that's for sure. Probably tomorrow, they tell me. I need to get home to my bed and my wife."

"I'm sure she's upset. Was she here?"

"No," Tommy answered. "My boy was here overnight. She was going to come this morning, but something came up. I'm sure she'll be by. You know, a thing like this makes you thankful for what you have. Like a good son, devoted wife, and the best damn oncology nurse in the country. Prettiest, too."

"Ah, well thanks," she said, blushing. "Well, Bobby found his way to me. I stopped over at Lukas' room just in time. Some big, stupid cop was leaning on him pretty good."

"Yeah," Tommy said. "I bet I know who that was. Carson. Major asshole."

"You'd think they'd be out looking for real bad guys. Like the one that stole my purse yesterday."

"Oh, no. How'd that happen, Carmen?"

"I had just cashed my paycheck at the credit union in the hospital lobby, so all my money was in it. I stopped at the bodega on Fifth, grabbed a twenty and ran in for a sec to get a quart of milk. I could swear I locked the car with the fob, but it must not have taken. Someone grabbed it right off the seat. I'm sure it was one of those seedy guys that are always hanging around outside of the place. They were both there went I went in, but gone when I came out."

"Damn. Yeah, I know the spot. Did you report it?"

"No. What good's that going to do? The only good cop I know is retired." She patted his hand. "I'll pull some overtime to make it up. They'll probably overdose on the dope they bought with my dough. I did love that purse, though."

"Send your old man, Buster, after them. He should be good for at least that much."

"Can't," she replied. "He's back in the joint. Burglary. I guess that's what the part-time job was that he said he got. I filed for divorce. I need an honest man, Tommy. Are there any left out there?"

"Just me," he said, half joking, half hopeful. Feeling drowsy, he took her hand. It was smooth and warm. He closed his eyes and enjoyed the silence and her presence, using his thumb to caress her palm as he slowly drifted into sleep.

His awareness came and went between the nurses coming to check on him and the dreams that passed through his subconscious like slowly moving ships. Eventually, he realized there was a woman sitting next to his bed. "Hello, Margie," he said, assuming his it was his wife, who was long overdue.

"Hi, Tommy. It's Diane."

He looked at her, momentarily confused.

"Diane," she repeated. "Your sister-in-law. Are you okay? Should I come back?"

He raised himself up a bit, the only formality he could manage from the confines of the hospital bed. "Hey, Diane. How's things? How's Jack?"

"Not bad, Tommy. I guess none of us can complain, seeing what's going on with you."

He sensed that she was downcast and nervous. She still wore her jacket and clutched her purse tightly on her lap.

"Are you going to be okay, Tommy?" she asked.

"Yeah, yeah. Don't worry about me. I'm getting out of here today or tomorrow. Pretty sure, anyway. Good as gold. I'll be home and pissing off your sister like always."

"I uh…I wanted to talk to you about something, Tommy. Maybe this isn't a good time." She looked toward the door.

"No, it's okay, Diane. What's on your mind, kid? I'm all ears."

"Well, I think something's been going on. Jack's been acting funny lately. Real distracted, you know? Fidgety. Making excuses to go out."

"Aw, it's probably just work. Don't jump to any conclusions."

She looked at the door again. "Well, there's more. A while back, Margie and I were just hanging out talking in my kitchen, when Jack came home. I dunno. I just felt something funny, like an intuition, the way they looked at each other, you know what I mean?"

Tommy sat up even straighter and waited for her to continue.

"And the thing is, Margie went upstairs to use the bathroom, don't ask why, but anyways instead of using the hall bathroom she went into the one off our bedroom. Something happened up there, we heard a crash, and she came downstairs and left in a hurry. I went up and found Jack's cologne spilled all over the place. He acted all weird about it."

"Jesus, Diane. That's a lot to process. She's a heavy drinker, you know that. Let's not jump to conclusions."

She started to cry. "I'm sorry, Tommy. I shouldn't have come here and dumped this on you, here in the hospital. I'm so sorry..." She pulled a tissue from the box on the stand attached to his bed and poured herself a glass of water from the flimsy plastic water pitcher that stood next to it.

"It's going to be okay. I'll get to the bottom of it, don't worry. Just let it go for now, and let me look into things. Don't do anything. Let's hope it's nothing, but you can be sure I'll find out either way. I'll let you know."

"Okay, Tommy. I'm sorry."

"Don't be sorry, Diane. You're good as gold, always were."

"Is she coming?"

"I don't know where Margie is. She was supposed to be here today, but I haven't seen her yet. Probably at the liquor store stocking up."

"I gotta go, Tommy. I gotta get back to work. I really just wanted to make sure you're okay."

"We go back a long way, don't we? I miss the old days, Diane. I really miss the old days. When everything was good, and fun. We didn't have too many problems back in the early years. Not compared to now, anyway."

She lingered for a while. They made awkward small talk until she left, and then he sat in silence, processing the news and slowly clenching and unclenching his hands. *I should've pulled the plug on her and this marriage a long time ago. Wasted time.*

He rang the nurse's buzzer, and when he came in Tommy asked for something for anxiety and sleep. He downed the pills with a large glass of water, then got up to black out the shades, returning to the bed to sleep.

The television came on, and he roused himself to clarity. There was another visitor in the chair: a short Asian man with jet-black hair tied in a topknot, and a black eye patch. The eye patch strap made a diagonal line across the man's forehead and down under his ear. The man sat looking at him without moving.

"Hey, Molletier," Tommy greeted him. "What are you doing here? You got treatments today, or just can't get enough of this dump?"

The man spoke in a slow, raspy tone. "Sensei. Call me 'Sensei,' as I asked you. It is Japanese, not the proper term for a Korean taekwondo master, but Americans do not know the difference, and the Korean version is hard for your people to say."

"Okay, okay. Got it," Tommy replied.

Molletier continued. "When we met in chemo a while back, you said you wanted to talk to me. I was here to see the doctor today, and I heard Nurse Carmen say you were here. Now I'm here. What do you want?"

Tommy remembered the man's blunt, emotionless attitude from their prior meeting. "Yeah, right. We talked about the old days when you were Bobby's instructor. How's things at the dojo?"

"The dojo is gone. No business these days. Parents just shove video screens in front of their kids to shut them up. They're all growing up weak and fat. No discipline."

Tommy reached for his remote and turned off the overhead TV. "I agree. I miss the old days. I bet it's not like that where your people come from. Where's that again, China?"

The man gave Tommy an even more hardened look. "Korea."

"Oh, right. Sorry. So how're you doing with the treatment? You did okay, keeping all that hair."

Molletier maintained his stony demeanor as he pulled up on the topknot, lifting the wig slightly from his scalp.

"Oh, sorry again."

"How is Bobby?" Molletier asked.

"Doing okay. He's having a rough time at work though. Some asshole's been picking on him. He's a sensitive guy, you know?" It was as far as Tommy could go toward revealing his son's recently disclosed homosexuality.

"I remember. Good boy. Big, strong. Respectful. He should have stayed in training. Send him to me. Private lessons."

"I'll run it by him. So what're you doing now that the studio is closed?"

"Private investigator work. Old job before taekwondo studio."

Tommy considered the possibilities. "Huh. You interested in doing a little work with me? I think I could use you on a couple of projects."

8 RECONCILIATION

OMMY FUSSED AS MARGIE TRIED to help him from the car and into the house. "I can do it. I can do it myself," he said testily as she tried to steady him.

When they were finally inside, she said, "I have the bed all ready for you up there. Go on up and relax. Put the TV on—and not the news, please!" she implored. "I'll bring you a sandwich and some soup."

"I'm not going to lay in the bed all the damn time, Margie. I'm fine. I got things to do." He used his muscled arms to help pull himself up the stairs toward the bedroom.

"You shouldn't drive, you know that. What if you have another seizure and get someone else killed?"

He reached the top landing with her trailing behind him. "Oh, but it's okay if I get *myself* killed?" he asked. "Jesus. I'm fine, I'm on the anti-seizure meds. I have shit to do."

"Rest tonight, please, Tommy. Maybe I'll go to Diane's later to give you some peace and quiet."

He turned and glared at her, suspicious that she might be off for a rendezvous. "I thought you were worried about me having another seizure? Who the hell is going to be here to stop me from choking on my puke?"

She appeared rattled by his question. "Okay, okay," she said. "I'll stay if that's what you want. Whatever helps."

The afternoon drifted into evening, as she occasionally appeared with full trays and disappeared with empty trays, doting on him to the extent he would allow. He lay in the bed, bored, fidgeting with the remote control and switching from one program to another.

He thought he heard her on the phone talking to someone, and quickly reached over and picked up the extension on the night-stand next to him, replacing it upon hearing the dial tone. He felt foolish. He tried not to let his mind drift to what she could be doing behind his back; to give her the benefit of the doubt. *Who could blame her if she did cheat on me, the way I used to be.* He wanted more than ever to make things right, at least for the time he had left. *Bobby's moving out. Maybe we can retire down South too.*

Night came, and she took longer than usual preparing for bed. He could hear her customary gargling—an attempt to rinse the alcohol from her breath. He had already showered and shaved, applying the aftershave that he always used to wear during their better times. After sleeping most of the afternoon, he felt rested. *Here goes nothing.*

She pulled back the sheets and eased in next to him. As was her habit, she turned on her reading light and picked up a magazine from the night table.

He slid over closer to her. "Listen, why don't you give that a break, for once. Let's talk. Let's watch something on TV together. Turn off the lamp, Margie."

She looked at him, discomfort and surprise on her face.

He wondered if she thought he was going to confront her. "Let's talk about good things, like the old days, and the future," he added.

She looked at him a moment, then replaced her magazine and switched off the light. In the process, she moved slightly away from him and folded her hands on her abdomen in the dark. "Okay, Tommy. What do you want to talk about?"

"Well," he started. "Bobby's not here much anymore. Gone again for the weekend. We're getting to be quite the empty-nesters, aren't we?" He slid a little closer to her and placed his hand on her thigh.

She didn't react to the gesture. "What do you think, Margie? Maybe we go for a fresh start— try to get the old magic back?"

She hesitated before speaking. "Tommy, you just got out of the hospital. You're not well. Why don't you rest? Let's wait until you're fully recovered." She patted his hand.

He could sense her discomfort with the idea, and the sting of rejection began to anger him. The thought of her past affair with his late partner came back to him, upsetting him further. "But if it was Paulie, no problem, right?"

She recoiled at the statement. "Don't you dare," she said sharply. She reached over and turned on the light. "How dare you!"

He was tempted to bring up his suspicion of her affair with his brother-in-law, but he checked himself. *Don't show your hand. Verify, then act.*

He climbed out of the bed and grabbed his pillow. "I'm gonna sleep in my office…for good," he said as he left the room.

He walked down the hall, pausing at their son's empty room. He stopped and went in. Moonlight shone through the window and illuminated Bobby's well-made bed and the mementos and artifacts of their life together on the shelves and walls. He looked at a large picture of them both standing in a stream, fishing poles in hand, wearing vests and hats adorned with lures. Another photo showed them in the woods, kneeling next to a dead buck, Bobby unsmiling and holding its head up to display the rack. Pictures of Bobby wearing football and hockey uniforms, striking standard sports poses, unsmiling. *I never really picked up that he wasn't enjoying those things like he should have been. He did it all for me. I wasted his life, trying to live vicariously through his youth.*

As he descended the stairs with a pillow and a blanket from the linen closet, he knew that he had crossed another bridge in his life, at least regarding his marriage. He felt as if he had been guided down a road during the past year, walking past everything he had known on his way, each thing crumbling to dust as he passed it by.

9 LAWYER UP

CARSON AND JACKSON WATCHED Lukas through the one-way mirror. He sat in the empty interview room, waiting and watching the clock on the wall. "They can't help but keep checking that clock," Carson said, laughing.

"I love making them wait, that must really suck," he continued. "You think this turkey is cooked yet, Jackson? Go back in and tell him it'll be just a little longer."

"As far as I'm concerned he is. I'd like to get out of here," Jackson answered, before doing as he was told.

Carson waited another twenty minutes, then entered the interview room from the hallway. He sat down across from Lukas and stared menacingly over the table. He tried to avoid looking toward the one-way mirror, knowing Jackson was behind it. "Thanks for coming in, Taylor. I see you're healing up nicely, at least enough to talk. Who bailed your ass out, anyway?"

"I'm sure you have that information," Lukas responded quietly.

Carson sized him up. *He's not stupid. Got some education. Not your normal street black.* He decided to switch strategy. *Good-cop time.* "Listen, Lukas. I can tell you're a smart guy. We have ways of making things work out here. You want something to drink or eat?"

"I'm good. Let's get this done so I can leave."

Carson shifted impatiently. "Like I said, you're smart. We can work things out without all the court bullshit. Your uncle is gone, nothing can bring him back. I'm sure he wouldn't want you wrapped up in all this…"

"Don't talk about my uncle. You didn't know him. He was a far better man than you."

The shot agitated Carson. "Yeah, I can tell by his rap sheet. Regardless, he loved you and wouldn't want you getting mixed up in this priest business. Not for protecting a whitey, right? C'mon, man. Be smart. Cooperate about Borata's involvement and all this other business goes away. He's sick—he'll die in jail. He won't be able to come at you."

Carson sat back to gauge the effect of his words. Lukas was silent, and Carson knew the wheels were spinning. *He's evaluating his options. Good.* He decided to add more pressure. "This all goes away. I can make sure nobody hassles you and your group going forward. We can all decide to live in peace and harmony, right?"

Lukas continued his silence. Carson leaned in and whispered, low enough that the microphones in the room wouldn't pick it up. "And I have ways to put you guys in business. You'd do very well, I promise. New motorcycles, the whole deal."

Lukas sat up straight and looked directly at the mirrored wall. "So, what you're saying, Detective Carson, is that you're a corrupt cop who can help us to make a lot of money by participating in illegal activities?"

Carson erupted in anger. "You know damn well that's not what I said, you fucker. Here I am trying to work with you, and you pull that shit, trying to ruin my reputation and career?"

"Don't you have to read me my rights?" Lukas asked calmly.

"You're damn right I do now. I'm done trying to work with you." He read Lukas his Miranda rights and waited for a response.

"I want a lawyer. Can't afford my own."

Carson laughed. "Good, that's what I was hoping to hear. Because those public defenders are a bunch of law school reject screw-ups. Our district attorneys eat them for lunch. You're looking at serious jail time, pal. Want to reconsider working with us? Last chance…"

"Lawyer."

As if on cue, a knock came at the interrogation room door. "Come in," Carson barked.

An officer opened the door, and a woman in a tailored suit walked in, briefcase in hand.

Carson tried to hide his reaction. *Oh shit. Jeanine Franconi.*

"Detective Carson," she said confidently. "Up to your old tricks, I see. Hassling the poor working people? Beats all that danger in chasing real criminals, right?"

"What're you doing here? This guy can't afford you. Still using your clients to make the payments on that sports car and mansion you live in up in the hills?" Carson asked.

"It's not your business who's paying me, Carson. Let's just say it's being taken care of by a friend. Let's get out of here, Lukas."

Carson remained silent as they prepared to leave. On the way out, she paused and said to Lukas, loud enough for Carson to hear, "Good thing your neighbor-lady upstairs grabbed her camcorder when she saw these guys pull up out front. This one's a slam-dunk for us."

She turned and smiled at Carson. "Have a good day, Detective. We'll expect the charges to be dropped by the end of the day. We'll let you know about our suit against the city and police department because of your behavior."

On his way out, Lukas turned toward Carson. "And, by the way, Tommy Borata is also a far better man than you," he added.

In the parking lot, Lukas asked, "Is that for real, what you said?"

"No," she answered. "I went around your neighborhood to check for security cameras and talked to some of the neighbors. I did talk to a Mrs. Irving, whose window faces the street in front of your place, and she seems to be quite a busybody. She said she saw some of it, so that was enough for me to go on. Carson is dumb. I've used similar tactics to bluff him before, but only when I knew he was pulling something shady. According to your neighbors, you're a solid citizen, Lukas."

"I'm trying. I'm sure trying," he answered.

10 CHEMO

THE SUBTLE, METHODICAL TICKING of the infusion console contrasted with the jagged sawtooth snores coming from the man next to Tommy. *I don't know which is worse.* He closed his eyes and tried to sleep, then opened them again, rechecking the clock on the wall and the level of fluid in the bag that was emptying into the vein in his arm. He looked down at the Eagle, Globe, and Anchor tattoo on his forearm. It seemed more faded each time he had to endure these treatments. His skin seemed paler and more shriveled, his former muscle tone slowly being eaten away.

He looked over at Molletier, sitting in the station previously occupied by his late friend Moses. Shutting his eyes again, he imagined himself back in time, hoping he could open his eyelids again and find Moses sitting in the chair, trading verbal jabs as they had often done. He imagined everyone he had known before in that pod, during his last rounds of chemo. They had a strong camaraderie—they were all strong together in the face of the inevitable. *Now they're all gone, except me.*

Another loud snort startled him, and he looked over at Molletier. He was sitting in the padded recliner, head back and mouth wide open. His black top-knotted wig was slightly askew. As Nurse Carmen walked by to check their consoles, Tommy asked, "Can't you do something about this guy's snoring? Isn't there some kind of drug?"

Carmen took a seat in the empty recliner on his other side. "Get some sleep, Tommy. You have another half hour or more. Don't forget your headphones next time."

"How the hell can I sleep with him sawing logs over here? He's on a maintenance dose, isn't he almost done? You got a rag you can put in his piehole until then?"

Carmen laughed and smiled at him, and it brought an immediate lift to his spirits. "How's things at home, Tommy?"

"Wonderful," he said sarcastically. "The old lady's got some side action going on, apparently. So I'm looking to move out. Other than that, aces." She looked at him sympathetically, and he felt bad about introducing negativity to the little time he got to spend with her. "But Bobby and I are doing great. Better than ever, in fact." He forced a smile at her.

She reached over and put a hand on his knee. "Hang in there. We're gonna get you through this round of chemo, then test for the mutation so we can get you onto the Forbaxatel. From there it'll be easy street. You're a good man, Tommy. You're gonna be okay. No matter what."

"Promise?" Tommy asked.

"Promise." She rose and winked at him before moving on. He watched her make the rounds, caring for each patient as if they were her own family, as Molletier's snoring continued. He scanned the surrounding seats in his pod, again wishing his old crew were all there. The only other occupied recliner contained a young boy, who stared straight at him. The boy was thin and pale, completely bald, with brilliant blue eyes that gave his appearance an alien quality. He wore a black bandanna featuring skulls and crossbones around his forehead. Tommy nodded, and the boy remained still, continuing to look at him without expression.

Tommy tipped his head back and gazed at the ceiling. The white aluminum gridwork held aged acoustic tiles. He wondered if they contained asbestos. *Pretty stupid thing to worry about, at this stage of the game.* He looked back over at the boy, who continued to stare, unblinking. Tommy closed his eyes again until nausea threatened to overtake him. His chills began to worsen, and he pulled his blanket tighter around him.

He checked again, and the boy was still watching him. He began to get annoyed. "What's your problem, kid?" he asked. The boy remained still. Tommy waved a hand. "Hello? Anyone in there?"

"Why don't you give her a kiss?" the boy asked.

"What?" Tommy responded.

"You heard me. Why don't you give her a kiss? You know you love her. That's *your* problem, old man."

"Whoa. Easy, kid. Don't be so hostile." Tommy grew uncomfortable, surprised that the kid was intimidating him. Molletier continued to snore, now a more rhythmic drone.

"When she comes back, why don't you kiss her and stick your tongue in her mouth. Then you can put your hand in her shirt and squeeze her big tits."

"Jesus. What are you, ten years old? That's not nice. Don't talk like that, kid. C'mon."

"Why don't *you* shut up, mister? What are you doing, sitting there feeling sorry for yourself? You're like ninety. You lived a long time and got to do all kinds of shit. I'm only eleven. Not even twelve yet. Only tits I've seen is in pictures. That's probably gonna be it for me. I won't be squeezing any melons."

"Where you looking at pictures like that? You're too young."

"My dad has a bunch of porno books in his closet. He thinks I don't know."

"You shouldn't be looking at those…"

Tommy was interrupted by Nurse Beulah. "What are you two boys talking about?" she asked.

The boy pointed at Tommy. "Something's wrong with that old guy. He keeps bothering me. He's talking about doing dirty stuff with that other nurse over there."

"What the—wait a minute..." Tommy sputtered.

Nurse Beulah laughed. "Nice try, Terry. I know this gentleman better than that. Tommy is a good guy. And I also know about your overactive imagination." She made some adjustments to the console, patted the boy on the head and moved on.

"What the hell was that?" Tommy asked the boy.

"Don't screw with me, Tommy. My dad's coming back soon, after his goddamn conference call is over, and he believes everything I say. He's got a guilty conscience, and I'm milking it for all I can get."

Tommy looked at the boy in disbelief. Molletier sputtered and coughed, choking on a particularly violent snore. He sat up, blinking.

"Good morning, sunshine," Tommy said, happy for the interruption.

"Nothing good about this," Molletier responded.

"You're lucky, it's just maintenance. Enjoy the remission, Sensei."

Molletier didn't respond. Carmen came over and began to disconnect and clean him up. "You two are both about done for today," she said.

"Thank God," Tommy said.

"That old guy said he wants to give you a big kiss," the boy interjected.

Carmen looked over at him while she began to remove Tommy's line and wipe his forearm with an alcohol-soaked cotton ball. "Really?" she asked.

"Yup, I swear," the boy responded. "He said a lot more than that, but I'm not allowed to say it."

Tommy started to correct him when Carmen leaned in and pressed her lips against his. They were soft and warm, slightly slippery from her lip gloss. He closed his eyes, and it seemed an eternity before she withdrew. He wanted to pull her back in immediately, as he hadn't experienced anything like that in a very long time. His heart raced dangerously.

They both looked at the boy, who appeared excited, and he finally smiled.

"See, I know how to make my patients happy," Carmen said to Tommy as she straightened up, motioning to the boy.

"You sure made this one happy, Carmen," Tommy responded. She smiled and moved on, and he looked over to Molletier, who was shaking his head. "You ready to get out of here, Sensei?"

They both rose and prepared to leave.

"Hey, Tommy. How about a shake from the cafeteria for your boy over here?" Terry asked.

"I guess you earned that," Tommy answered. "What flavor, kid?"

11 IMPROMPTU DOJO

SENSEI MOLLETIER WALKED DOWN the ranks of the two lines of students. They stood in rigid fighting poses as he checked the sturdiness of their form and made slight adjustments to their positioning. "Strong in form, strong in mind," he barked. He threw punches and kicks at their frozen arms and legs to demonstrate his point. He looked fearsome with his eye-patch and black instructor's uniform, his black belt decorated with bright gold Korean lettering.

Molletier threw a lightning-fast kick toward Lukas' groin, stopping just short and then snapping it back. "Best place to strike a man is there. Most sensitive place. Also, penis is root of all evil, responsible for downfall of society." The group laughed.

"You got that right, Sensei," Tass shouted. "What about a woman, though?"

"Woman is perfect. No weak spots."

"Damn right, sir!" she responded, as the men grumbled.

A group of motorcycles were lined up in the parking lot as uniformly as the students who owned them. Tommy watched from a nearby park bench, wrapped in blankets despite the warm morning. He wouldn't have missed it, despite the opportunity to be home in bed. He put his feet up on the cooler of ice and water bottles that they had kiddingly charged him with guarding, and took in the scene.

It brought him back to the many evenings he'd supervised his son's taekwondo lessons through a glass partition in Molletier's school. The same instructions were issued in the same authoritative voice, although it was somewhat less powerful these days. *It's hitting him too, the damage from this disease and from the treatment. He's where I was last year, still strong but fading.*

This time, the dojo was open-air rather than in the humid, sweat-soaked studio. The students all wore black vests which read 'Black Eagles Motorcycle Club.' Molletier ran them through a series of blocks, punches, and kicks, their shouts and grunts filling the air in unison. *Wish I could go back. Let the kid off the hook. I just wanted him to be tougher, ready for this cruel world.*

He let the memories pass, returning himself to the present. He looked around at the brilliant colors of the natural setting: the blue sky dotted with white clouds, trees and grass in beautiful shades of green, multicolored flowers in the gardens area nearby. He took in a deep breath of fresh air and listened beyond the sounds of the lesson to focus on the birds calling to each other from the surrounding trees. *It really is a beautiful planet.*

He watched as a woman exited a car with a fast food bag in her hand and approached the nearby concrete block restrooms. As she passed near a trash can, she launched the bag. It bounced off the rim and fell to the sidewalk, dumping its contents. The woman paused to look at it and then walked into the ladies' room. *We're the only stain on this world. I wonder how we got here. Somehow, we don't fit in with everything else.* He struggled to remove the blankets and rose to take care of the trash.

Molletier spilled out a box full of pads and instructed the group to don them and pair off to spar. Tommy watched as they attacked each other with vigor, taunting one another playfully but striking serious blows. The slaps of the gear, along with grunts and laughs, came continuously.

Lukas was sparring with Tass, and she appeared to be getting the better of him, using her shorter stature to strike his thighs with repeated kicks from close range, taking away his reach advantage. He was clearly still tender from the rough ride, and his mobility was limited.

"Bring it, girl, bring it oooon!" Lukas called to her. He went into a mock Mohammad Ali shuffle and tapped her on the top of the head, angering her.

"Let's be serious, people," Molletier called sternly. "Taekwondo is serious business!"

Tass lunged in and drove several punches toward Lukas' midsection, pulling up short to avoid hurting him. He grabbed her in a bear-hug, wrestling her to the ground and kissing her. She wrapped her legs around him and kissed him back. "Easy girl, I'm still all busted up," he said.

Molletier looked over to Tommy, shaking his head. Tommy thought he detected a rare smile on the man's face. More chills ran through Tommy's body, and he started to feel dizzy and nauseous. He began to fear another seizure; he'd been worried about it since being back in the park. He hoped they'd wrap it up soon so he could get home and warm up.

Tommy closed his eyes and thought of ways to spend quality time with Bobby. *He likes drawing and painting. Maybe I could take it up myself. I might have some hidden talent there.* He envisioned himself in the same park, standing at an easel, dabbing away at a canvas, with a beret on his head, capturing the landscape. The picture made him laugh, which set off a coughing attack.

"You okay there, Pops?" Lukas asked. The Eagles had finished their lesson and were standing by politely waiting for him to take his feet off the cooler. He did so, and they dove in eagerly.

"You guys are wearing me out just watching you," he answered.

Molletier walked up with the cardboard box of gear. "Good progress, students. Much more work needed. Taekwondo requires much time, much discipline, much practice."

"Thank you, Sensei," Tass said to him, bowing. The others followed suit, and Molletier appeared pleased. "Each Saturday and Sunday morning, we will meet here for practice. Students are committed?" he asked. The group agreed with enthusiasm.

They rested for a while, taking in the serene environment. "There you go, Tommy. You've got your own ninja army," Lukas said.

Tommy liked the thought. "Imagine, we could really start to clean up some of the bad neighborhoods. Except for all these punks carrying guns now," he added wistfully.

"Here comes trouble," Tass said, looking over toward the parking lot. A dark sedan had pulled up next to the motorcycles. Carson and Jackson emerged and began looking over the bikes, pointing things out to one another. Jackson had a ticket book and pen in his hand and began to write.

"Got to be a special place in hell for people that miserable," Tommy said.

The two cops strode confidently over to the silent group. "Who's got the Suzuki?" Carson asked, smiling.

"That's me," Tass responded.

"Registration sticker's out of date. Here, you go." He tore a ticket from the booklet that Jackson handed him and offered it to her.

She grabbed it from his hand. "I got the new sticker at home, didn't put it on the bike yet. Can't you cut me a break on that?"

"Tell it to the judge, sister," Carson laughed.

"I'm not your damn sister, buddy," she said, rising from the picnic bench she sat on. The others rose up as well.

"Easy, Tass," Lukas said. "We'll take care of this in court. You done here, *officers*?"

"'Detectives' to you, Taylor," Carson sneered at him.

Jackson had been looking at the box of pads. He bent over and poked around in it. "What's this, kung-fu class? You people running some kind of illegal business here on public grounds? Who's in charge of this mess?"

Molletier came around from the back of the group and picked the box up, placing it out of reach on the picnic table. "I am in charge. This is free public group exercise in the park. No money. No business transaction."

Carson looked at Jackson. "Jackson, get a load of Bruce Lee over here—eye patch, topknot and all. Halloween's a few days out, and this joker has his costume on already." The cops both laughed.

"Fuck you, Carson," Tommy said in a weak voice. Carson walked around them to see who'd addressed him.

"Well, well. If it ain't Tommy Borata. Or is it the former Tommy Borata? Damn, tough guy, you're looking pretty sorry, all shriveled up like an old man in those blankets. You're wasting away fast, pal. Hang on at least until I can put you away, alright?"

Lukas moved directly in front of Carson until they were nose-to-nose. "Back off. If your business is done here, leave us alone."

Carson put a finger on Lukas' chest. "Another tough guy. You want another ride, Taylor? I'll really try to check the seat belt this time, promise. Sort of." He laughed again.

"Please leave us. Now," Molletier said firmly. He pulled Lukas back with one arm, stepping into his place in front of Carson.

Carson reddened, the smile disappearing from his face. "Listen, you gook…" he started, grabbing the front of Molletier's dobok top.

In an instant, Molletier moved like a precision machine, breaking Carson's hold and stepping back, throwing a kick into Carson's chest, knocking him backward and to the ground.

"You motherfucking chink bastard," Carson raged, getting up to charge. Jackson grabbed him and held him back.

"We can't, Carson. No cause. It'll turn out bad. Too many people around. Let it go, for now."

Carson shook him off, seething. "Alright, alright. You assholes will be hearing a lot more from me, and soon. Keep your head up, all of you. Especially you, Borata. I'm coming for you.

And you, Charlie Chan. You better hope your papers are in order."

"Molletier," the sensei responded. "Sensei Molletier."

The two cops spun and headed back to their car, as the Eagles offered quiet high-fives and back slaps to each other and Molletier.

Tommy smiled from his bench. "Let's get the hell out of here, gang, while the gettin's good. Lunch is on me."

12 COWBOY CARSON

CARSON PUSHED HIS MUG toward the bartender for a refill. The twang of old country music filled the tavern, and the patrons at the tables and barstools seemed content in their environment. The walls were lined with the skeletal heads and horns of large animals, and a massive Confederate flag was pinned to the ceiling at all four corners. Below the flag, large timber beams spanned from wall to wall, and brassieres hung where they'd been tossed over the years by inebriated customers.

"We're not going to get anything outta that Lukas Taylor dude," he said. "He's pretty defiant. Those fuckers stick together pretty tight." He looked at himself in the bar-back mirror and felt that he looked just right in the setting. He lowered the brim of his Stetson and unbuttoned his top shirt button to expose more chest.

Jackson drained his mug and placed it next to Carson's. "Agreed. I think he'd give Borata up though, if he wasn't so closely tied to his Uncle Moses. What're you going to do about the charges on Taylor?"

"I didn't write him up. Nobody else knew about the plant except you and me, so that part was easy. I told the chief that we worked it out."

"Thank God for that. I wasn't looking forward to the paperwork. How do you know Taylor's not gonna push back? Borata had him lawyer up—he might see a big payday coming if they decide to sue."

"Nah," Carson said. "Taylor's too principled. I apologized to him man-to-man. He seemed to appreciate that, and I told him I'd make sure we'd stay out of his group's way.

"I'm thinking about leaning on Borata's kid instead. It's more fun, anyway. I have a suspicion about him. I think he's a fag, and I got a tip about a place he might be hanging out."

He looked over at the redhead two stools down, who was now sitting alone.

"Hey there, sweetie. My name is Carson. Where'd your old man go?"

She looked over to him drowsily, drained the shot in front of her, and then the one from the place where the man had been sitting. "He's in the shitter. What's it to ya?"

"Damn, little lady. You have a good buzz going on for this early on a Sunday. I guess I'd have to get loaded too if I was with a loser like that dude. Why don't you give me your number?"

"Fuck off, mister." She returned her gaze to the bar and reached for the half-mug of beer in front of her.

Jackson laughed. "Oh man, Carson. That's rich. She told you. It's not often I see you get shot down like that."

"Shut the fuck up, Jackson." Carson returned to the image of himself in the mirror.

The man came back and ordered refills for himself and the woman.

"Paul," the woman said to him. "That man there wants my number. Says his name is Carson."

"Uh-oh, here we go," Jackson said under his breath.

The man turned to Carson, who remained facing forward. They were inches from each other on the adjacent barstools. "Buddy, you been asking my wife for her number?"

Carson remained silent and still. He imagined himself, as he always did in these situations, as a gunfighter in an Old West saloon, or at least the version he'd seen in countless Western movies.

"He got no respect for you, Paul. Not for you, or me," the woman added.

Paul raised his voice. "I mean, clearly she's wearing a wedding ring. You had to see it. Don't you check at least, before hitting on a woman?"

"Let's go," Jackson said to Carson. Carson didn't budge.

"The nerve, right, Paul?" the redhead continued.

Paul looked across the bar to the image of Carson looking at himself in the mirror. He waited for a response, and then pushed lightly on Carson's shoulder. "Excuse me…" was all he managed to get out.

Carson grabbed the man's wrist before he could withdraw it, then swept from his barstool and forced the man to the floor in a single motion. He spun, flipped his adversary over, and yanked the man's arm between both legs into an arm-bar. "Yee-ha," he yelled.

Paul screamed in agony, and the drunk woman worked to get off her stool. Jackson got up and rushed to keep her from jumping onto Carson's back.

The bartender hustled down from the other end of the bar. "Knock it off, dammit. Carson, let him go. Not in my damn bar, please. I've asked you before."

Carson relaxed and got up, laughing. Jackson retrieved his hat from the floor and handed it back to him. The man got up, flexing his arm, and took a step toward Carson. "What the fuck was that, asshole? How about a fair fight, man to man?"

"Take it outside," the bartender warned again. "Out of my bar with that bullshit."

"Let's go then, tough guy," Carson said. "It's what I live for."

Jackson pulled his wallet and showed his badge behind Carson's back. Paul noticed it, and immediately changed his demeanor. "C'mon," he said to his wife. "Give me your keys. I'll drive, I should be okay. You're hammered."

She fumbled in her purse as they made their way to the door. "You're an asshole," she said to Carson. "Fake-ass concrete cowboy in some city bar, think you're somethin' you're not. Asshole, that's what you are."

They left, and Carson moved to the window to watch. After they entered their vehicle, he pulled out his cell phone and dialed.

"Yeah, it's Carson. You out on patrol today? Good. Listen, I'm in Shooters over here on Fifteen. Some guy just went out to his car shit-faced and got behind the wheel. Wouldn't listen to me. Try to get over here and pick him up for DUI before he gets too far down the road. He's with his old lady; she's a smart-ass, too. Don't take any shit from her, she's loaded. You might have to take them both in. Green Chevy Impala."

He snapped his phone closed. "Some people never learn," he said, smiling at the bartender and Jackson. "You mess with the bull, you get the horns." Both shook their head at him in disgust.

13 PURSE SNATCHERS

YOU GOT ANY FAMILY, SENSEI?" Tommy asked as they drove through the city streets.

"Mother and father both died in Korea. Wife left," he answered in his solemn tone. "She went back to Korea. Daughter moved west, to LA, and died from drugs." He paused at that and was silent for a time. "It's just me now," he finally added. "Alone."

"How's your treatment coming along? Anything new?"

"Still clear for now, but I feel a change coming. The treatments only make me sicker, weaker. Korean medicine, old natural herbal medicine, is better. Maybe I need to stop the modern treatments, and use only Korean medicine."

"You might have something there, buddy," Tommy said. "Where can I get some of that? Can't hurt, right?"

They took a detour to the Korean section of the city, and Molletier brought him to a small shop. The female proprietor seemed to Tommy to be incredibly old. *Ancient. Wise.* Molletier spoke to her in their native language while Tommy browsed the shelves. The place itself felt timeless and exotic. It smelled of things he'd never experienced—of mysteries older than the planet itself.

They called him over, and she led him to a back room, indicating that he should lie down on a massage-type table. "Hey, wait a minute…" he said to Molletier.

"Do not insult her with that," he responded before Tommy could finish. "Foolish American, mind always in the gutter."

"No, I mean, we're not going to do any of that acupuncture stuff, are we? I don't like needles."

"Just examination," Molletier said.

Tommy complied. The woman stood over him, looking deeply into his eyes, examining his mouth and tongue with a flat wooden tool. She moved her hands over his body, pressing gently in different places, focusing on the areas where his organs were, prodding through his clothing. She removed his shoes and socks and spent a long time working his ankles and feet.

She completed her work and motioned for him to get down. After a short conference with Molletier, he said, "She says you're a very sick man," and then laughed, exposing his sarcasm.

"Oh, thanks a lot. I could've looked in the mirror to figure that out," Tommy said.

The proprietress was moving among her shelves, selecting items and packaging them up. She brought a small bag to the register and rang it up. "Seventeen dollar," she said.

"Oh, she speaks English now, at the cash register, right?" Tommy said, opening his wallet and extracting a credit card.

"She only speaks English money. To run the store," Molletier said. "Cash only."

As they continued the drive, Molletier said, "One teaspoon of powder in your tea, morning and night. Take the pill morning, noon, and night."

"I don't drink tea, I drink coffee."

"Not any more. Only tea; green tea. Add the powder."

Oh brother. They reached their destination, and Tommy pulled the car over. "You got the plan down, Sensei?" he asked. They peered down the street through the windshield. It was dusk and the few streetlights that were working provided just enough light to see their destination.

"You see the bodega there on the right side? Those two guys standing out front are the guys we're looking at. They're always there. Couple of fucking bums. I'm sure they're the ones that took Carmen's purse."

"I understand the plan," the sensei said calmly.

"Like we discussed, go around behind the building. They'll probably head right up that alley next to it. Be waiting for them at the end. I'll come in from the other end, and we'll have them trapped. I'm sick and weak, but I have my Taser to handle one of those skinny junkies if you can hold the other one. They won't offer much resistance. Let's just rough them up and hold them. I want to ask questions, see if I can get some of her cash back."

"I understand the plan," the sensei repeated.

"Go easy. Don't kill anyone, for chrissakes."

"I understand the plan."

"This will work, Sensei. This ruse, the role I'm gonna play, is something I learned from my old friend Moses—good guy, the best." He paused a moment to reflect and then thought better of letting his emotions take control of him. "Okay, Sensei. Let's move. Go ahead."

Molletier exited the car and moved stealthily across the street and behind the row of buildings.

Tommy looked in the rearview mirror to make sure he appeared properly disheveled. He loosened the tie around his neck, then opened the car door and crouched down to exit discreetly. *I'll make you proud, Moses.*

He crossed in the middle of the block, rather than using the crosswalk. Making his way down the sidewalk toward the bodega, he alternated his pace and swayed just enough to be convincing. He felt the eyes of the two men on him as he brushed past them and entered the store.

He ordered a bottle, still in character.

"You drunk?" the young clerk asked. "I'm not supposed to sell to drunks."

Tommy pulled his billfold, flashing his shield as he pulled out a twenty. The clerk rang up the purchase without commenting further.

As he exited, he waved a liquor bottle in a brown paper bag at the men in front and said, "Happy happy hour, my brothers." He intentionally stumbled on the steps and grabbed the railing for emphasis. Pausing before crossing the street in front of them, he feigned a struggle to place his wallet back into his back pocket. It fell to the sidewalk as he stepped off the curb and crossed the street.

After reaching the other side, he turned to continue down the sidewalk, checking out the front of the store in his peripheral vision. As he expected, the two men were already gone.

He crossed back over the street quickly, stepping up his pace as he neared the mouth of the alley next to the store. He was already breathing hard and exhausted, but the adrenaline and excitement from his days of doing this as a cop propelled him onward. *I'm a hunter again, on the scent of the prey.*

14 RECRUITMENT

IT WAS A LONG WAY to the other end of the alley, and much darker there. As his compromised body brought him closer as quickly as it could, Tommy could make out movement. He heard the sounds of grunts, yells cut short, and swishing clothing. One sound he remembered from the long past—the K'ihap attack cry of Korean taekwondo.

By the time he reached them, only Molletier was left standing. The other two men lay sprawled and groaning on the ground, and he could make out the sheen of fresh blood on their faces. "Stay down. Stay on the ground," Tommy commanded, pulling the Taser from the holster under his jacket.

Molletier had just retrieved his top-knot wig from the ground and was placing it back on his head. "Here's your wallet," he said, holding it out to Tommy.

"That's the decoy; it only had a few bucks in it," Tommy answered, taking it. He extracted the bills and threw the empty wallet at one of the thieves. He pulled his shield from his own wallet again and stuck it in the face of one of the men, then the other. "We're undercover. Where's the purse you took from a woman's car out front the other day?"

"Back there, in the dumpster, if it ain't been picked up by sanitation yet," one of the men said. Molletier headed toward it.

"The cash? What about the cash?" Tommy asked.

"Gone. We spent it. I'm sorry…"

His words were interrupted by Tommy's kick to his ribs. He felt his anger take him over, and picked the man's head up and smacked it into the alley. He moved to the other man.

The man crawled up against the building and cowered. "Don't, please. It was him, he did it all. I didn't get nothing…"

Tommy's boot found his ribs as well. He bent down and yanked his head up by the hair. As the man began to scream in protest, Tommy's wrist was grabbed from behind.

"No more. Let's go," Molletier said. He was holding the purse in his other hand.

Tommy addressed the second man. "We'll leave it at this, but let me tell you, don't *ever* take another person's purse or wallet again. You do, or if you make a big deal out of this lesson, and we'll be back, and next time, no mercy. Capisce?"

"Yeah, yeah," the man said. The other simply nodded slightly. Blood was spreading below his head, onto the grease and broken glass of the alley floor.

"Do yourself a favor and stay put for a few minutes. There's a squad car out on the street. They'll leave if you hang back a bit," Tommy lied. He tilted his head to the mouth of the alley, indicating Molletier should follow him out.

He didn't want to go to the car just yet, in case their curious behavior had been observed. He led Molletier through the city, zig-zagging over a few blocks until he reached his destination—Wyla's Bar.

When they were inside and settled at the bar, he motioned to the bartender. Although they were the only patrons who weren't black, some of the others signaled a greeting to Tommy.

"The usual for me, Luc," he said. "What'll you have, Sensei?"

"Beer," Molletier replied.

"What kind?" Lucius asked.

"Tap. Anything," Molletier responded.

Lucius looked at the two of them. "Damn, Borata. We're getting to be a real United Nations around here, thanks to you." Tommy wasn't sure if he was kidding or not. It was always hard to tell because of the barkeeper's icy demeanor and dry sense of humor.

Molletier didn't seem to care. Tommy figured the sensei had probably been subjected to the same kind of wisecracks, prejudice, and hatred that the other patrons of the bar were used to. The same kind of jokes he'd made himself once upon a time, back in the safe, white environment of the station house and squad car. *In this white world. Before I became a better person.*

"So, ah, Sensei. I thought you said you understood the plan?"

"I understood the plan."

"What happened to the part about holding them up until I could get there and talk to them, put a little scare in them?"

"They were scared already. I didn't want them to run back at you and hurt you. They were bad guys—I took care of business. Problem solved. I like to hurt the bad guys."

"I can handle myself, don't worry about that," Tommy said. "Plenty of experience. We got to stick to the plan if we're going to work together, though. Okay?"

"I understand," Molletier said.

Lucius delivered their order, and Molletier took a long drink from his mug. He looked over at Tommy. "No beer for you?"

"Nah. I gave it up. Long time ago. Wasn't good for me. I wasn't a nice guy back then, and I was much, much worse when I got into that stuff. I'm on a health kick," he laughed. "Health kick with stage-four cancer."

"So, who's next?" Molletier asked him.

The bluntness of the comment took Tommy by surprise. Despite his concern about the plan not being followed, he admitted to himself that it was impressive watching Molletier dismantle the two men so quickly. *It was like a damn Bruce Lee movie. This guy is a weapon.*

"Good question. I was a cop, but one thing I hate is bad cops. Cocky, aggressive, dishonest bad cops. Cops are like priests—there's nothing better than a good one; nothing worse than a bad one. It's a trust and responsibility that should never be abused. One we both know is a real jerk-off. He's crooked and racist."

"I hate cops," Molletier added.

"Whoa. I told you I was a cop, right?"

"Yeah. Bad cop, I think you said."

"Okay, okay. Got it. Jesus. Anyway, this guy won't be so easy. He's some kind of MMA guy, what is it—mixed martial arts?"

"It is garbage. No integrity, no dignity. Showoff bullshit. It's not from the source—Shaolin. Taekwondo is more than fighting. It's about discipline, character, perseverance, courtesy. That other stuff, it's like pro wrestling. Bunch of loud mouth clowns."

It was the most Tommy had ever heard the man say at one time. "Sheesh. So I guess you're in. But can you handle someone like that? He's a big motherfucker, and nasty."

Molletier only stared at him in response. "Even weak from treatment, I'm strong in taekwondo and strong in my mind," he finally said. "Like you, I don't have much to lose, and I don't have much time."

1 CARSON'S FOLLY

DON'T PULL INTO THE PARKING LOT," Carson said. "Drop me at the vacant warehouse next door, and I'll walk over. Sorry man. I don't want my car in this lot, it's too conspicuous."

"The shit I do for you, playing chauffeur on my night off," Jackson responded. "So, you sure you're going to need a ride back, or you planning on scoring tonight?" He punched his partner playfully in the arm, causing the car to swerve slightly.

"Careful, asshole. The last thing we need is to get pulled over heading to a gay club, with me in this getup and coke in the glove box. I'll spend a few hours casing the place, looking for any back room drug-dealing or worse yet, pay for play.

Maybe start a few conversations to see if I can lure anyone to act as a snitch. Then I'll call for a lift back. I'm gonna need a long hot shower after mingling with a bar full of sweaty faggots."

Jackson pulled the car over, and Carson opened the glove box, removing a small vial of cocaine. He prepared a hit for himself and snorted it, then got out of the car, placing a ten-gallon hat on his head. "Put that away for me, will you?" he asked Jackson as he closed the car door and headed for the club.

Jackson lowered his window and shouted, "Hey, you look like that guy in the Village People," and drove off.

The comment irritated Carson, and he thought about bailing out on the idea, but the tingling of his senses and the anticipation were too strong. They propelled him toward the door. It was an idea that he'd kicked around in his head for a long time, and now that he was finally going to execute it, his adrenaline was flowing strongly.

The muffled, pounding music and garish neon lights across the parking lot were drawing him in, and he had to work to keep his steps measured.

Don't want to appear too anxious. Act like you're a regular at these things, just from out of town.

"Howdy, pardner," someone called out.

He turned his head and saw a fat older man in a Captain Kangaroo costume approaching the door from the other side of the lot.

"I'm single tonight too. I like the big, strong, rugged types. Want to hang out inside?" the man continued.

Carson froze. He felt a confused mix of emotions. Anger and embarrassment won out. "Buzz off, fatso." He paused and waited for the man to enter, then took a moment to compose himself before going through the door.

~*~

Disco-ball lights splayed the room and added to the festive atmosphere. Seventies dance music blared, and Bobby was happy in his element as he sat at the bar taking it all in. "I love Halloween. You make a pretty good Clint Eastwood, Mike," he said to his companion on the next seat.

"Thanks, Bobby. I don't know about that Bozo costume, though."

"Yeah, it's pretty ridiculous. I wanted the last thing anyone would recognize me in." Bobby fluffed the huge plumes of orange hair that stood out from the sides of his mask. "Wearing this mask sucks. What a pain in the ass."

Mike laughed. "I bet. Well, keep it on at least until the contest. I think you have a shot."

Bobby scanned the place, looking for other friends. The gay bar was an oasis, the only place in the city where he could be himself. He watched as other couples happily interacted, and wondered what the world would be like if everyone was accepted for who they were. *Who they were born as.*

He looked back at Mike. "Hey, you know how I was saying how my dad has changed? That we talked it out and he's cool with everything now?"

"Yeah," Mike answered. "I'm not sure I'm buying it. All I know is he's got quite a reputation for being a hard-ass cop. He was in the Marines too, right?"

"No, it's true. I told him I'm moving in with someone. I didn't say who. I think it's time, Mike. I want to bring you over, to meet him and my mom." It was something he had yearned for,

for a very long time. Just the mention of taking this step made him tingle with excitement. It made him happy, and he signaled a passing bartender for another round for them both.

Mike hesitated. "Wow, well, that's a big step. Maybe someday we can be out—be normal like other people. All of these other oppressed groups, they go through hell too, but at least they can live their lives openly. Not us, though. It sucks."

"It's kind of hard to hide it if you're black or Hispanic," Bobby laughed. "Easier if you're gay. But anyway, that one small step, to be able to be ourselves in my house, around my family, would be like a dream. Then maybe we could work toward moving somewhere away from here."

"Yeah, like Key West, or the California coast," Mike added. "How great would that be? A fresh start, nobody being judgmental, we could just be ourselves. No hiding. Right, like a dream."

"I know we could find jobs. We could live on the cheap, too," Bobby said. "Fresh start. I could get out of the cop business, do something I love and enjoy. Imagine our lives without all the job stress and hiding who we are all the time. It'd be…nirvana."

"I could write, and you could paint," Mike mused. "You're right. What's more important—a lot of money, killing yourself for a career you hate, or happiness every single day? It sounds too good to be true. But I guess it's like when you're on vacation and talk about living at the beach or whatever. Everyone talks about it, but when you get home, back in the grind, it's forgotten, and nobody ever really does it. Dreams."

"That's the thing, Mike," Bobby said excitedly. "Who do *we* want to be? The people like that, or the ones that actually make it happen? We can *do* this, I know we can. Let's just go for it—start planning now, and make it our goal for a year from now. A year from today."

Mike looked into his drink as if the answer were there. "I guess I'm willing to give it a go if you are, Bobby. Anything's better than these sad, hidden gay clubs. It's hard to relax even here. I keep waiting for the door to burst open and the right-wing militia to come in and arrest us all for being subversive perverts or something. With the rise of the conservatives and the religious right, it's like we're going back to the fifties or something. That crazy politician that's been in the news—Brand—he scares me."

"I guess the fifties weren't a bad time if you were a straight, white, Christian male," he laughed. "Anyway, that settles it," Bobby said. "We're doing this. Step one with my parents, and step two getting the hell out of Dodge. You and me, cowboy Clint!" He punched Mike in the arm for emphasis.

From the corner of his eye, Bobby picked up a tall, muscular man making his way across the dance floor, headed in their direction. He was dressed in garish Western gear, wearing a fake mustache, large aviator sunglasses, and an oversized cowboy hat. As he crossed the floor, he shoved away dancers who moved into his path. Despite the costume, Bobby recognized him immediately. *Carson.*

"Mike, real quick. This guy coming toward us, he's trouble. He's a cop in my precinct. He's not gay. He's not here to have fun...at least I don't think so. He's probably here for trouble. He's looking for me, or he wants to take this place down. Don't talk to him if he comes over."

~*~

Carson couldn't stand the thought that he was breathing in their sweat, touching them. *Faggots.* A well-built man, dressed as a western serape-wearing High Plains Drifter, caught his eye. A spot at the bar opened next to him. *I need a fucking beer.*

As he reached it, he squeezed in. "How's it going, Clint? Buy you a drink?" he asked the man next to him. The man stared into his drink and didn't answer. Carson signaled a bartender and ordered a beer and a shot.

"Excuse me. I said how's it going, Clint Eastwood?" He waited. "I saw Bozo here a minute ago. Where the fuck did Bozo go?" He laughed and became annoyed that the man didn't appreciate his humor.

"Had to make a phone call," Mike finally responded.

"You two seem like a mismatch. He looked pretty fat to me; from a distance, anyway. I like your getup. I'm a big Clint fan. The Duke, too."

Carson found himself experiencing strange, conflicting emotions, balancing the role he was playing against his homophobic self-image. He felt he was losing control of one in favor of the other. "You want to catch a flick sometime?"

Mike didn't answer, and Carson's irritation rose. "Why're you being rude? Don't like tough guys? You like the sissy ones?"

"Sorry. I don't feel good," Mike said.

"You being smart with me, boy?"

Mike had finally had enough. He looked over at Carson. "Why are you here if you aren't gay?" he asked.

"Who says I'm not gay?" Carson asked.

"That's the way you're coming off," Mike answered.

"Well, maybe your *gaydar* needs adjusting."

"Maybe *you* need to be honest with yourself," Mike said, finally looking him in the eye.

Carson downed the shot and gave up on the rest of his beer, slapping Mike on the back of the head as he left. "See you later, asshole." He headed toward the bathroom. *I hate to go here, but I got to piss like a racehorse.* He pushed through the crowd, toward the overhead sign for the men's room.

He entered the bathroom and stopped immediately. A man stood at a urinal, wearing a Bozo costume, holding the mask in one hand. Carson's spirits suddenly swelled, as they always did when he cornered prey, particularly when it was an unexpected bounty. "Well, well. If it ain't Bozo Bobby Borata."

The man looked over at him in shock, and the color drained from his face. Carson smiled in response. He took up the urinal next to Bobby and slapped him on the back, forcing him into the porcelain. "How's it hanging, Bobby? I'm here for work, of course, but I don't imagine you are."

Bobby dropped the mask and zipped up quickly, almost running out the door.

16 SUSPECT

TOMMY WAITED IMPATIENTLY while Carson reviewed the papers he'd taken out of the folder in front of him. Sitting still for a long period in the uncomfortable chair was exacerbating everything going wrong inside of him. The constant cold and weariness from his disease and treatment were growing, and he had nothing to distract himself from them.

He became aware that he was picking at the cuts that had appeared on his fingertips, making them bleed, and working his tongue over the sores that had developed in his mouth. His stomach was roiling, burbling, and he felt his nausea growing. He was well aware from his long experience that this was all done for a purpose. The waiting, the thermostat adjusted to make even a healthy person uncomfortable.

"Can we get on with this, Carson?" he asked. "It's late, and I like to get to bed early."

Carson ignored him, continuing to flip through pages of notes and casually drinking a cup of coffee. Finally, he put the papers back in the folder and looked up. "Thanks for coming in, Mr. Borata," he said in an official tone.

"Cut the shit, asshole," Tommy replied. "I don't have all day, so get to the point. I'm a sick man, you know." He looked around the interview room, familiar with it from the many times he had sat on the other side of the desk, or behind the one-way glass on the wall.

"Not too sick, right?" Carson said, now looking him directly in the eyes. "You and your friend, Moses, the um, n…"

"Don't say it, I'm warning you," Tommy cut in.

"Right, the *black guy. African-American.* You two were getting around pretty good for a couple of sick dudes. I've got a dead priest to show for it."

"I got nothing to do with that. Moses went rogue. You saw his confession."

"I'm still not convinced. I think you two had a *plan* before he 'went rogue.' That's conspiracy on your part, Borata. But hey, guess what? You're sick, and medical care is free in prison. Bonus." He laughed, to accentuate his point. "And now, you're running around with some crazy one-eyed gook—Molletier, right? Now that you're heading for your judgment, you're all about loving the freak show out there, aren't you? Do you think that's going to make a difference after all the shit you did when you were a cop? And you're judging me, Borata?"

Tommy recognized the tactic. Carson was trying to get him to lose his cool and say something he'd regret. He ignored him and tried to find a comfortable position. "You had to go after the kid, right, Carson? Lukas? He's a good kid—doesn't even drink or do drugs. You're a fucking disgrace to that badge for what you did. He's twice the man you are, and so was his uncle."

Carson looked up and offered a smirk. "Yeah...that was just an oversight. Defective buckles in that old piece-of-shit paddy-wagon. You know that. You've been there before, right? Taken a few perps for a rough ride yourself, haven't you, Borata?"

"Let's not wander through the past, Carson. I'm not feeling well. You don't want a shitload of puke to clean up in here, do you?"

He had Carson's attention. Tommy had gauged him as the kind of tough guy who would have trouble with that sort of thing. He realized that he was suppressing flatulence, holding his cheeks together out of habit, and wondering why he was bothering. He released it.

Carson disregarded the question. "You ready to talk to me about the priest thing? I can cut you a good deal. Your buddy did the heavy lifting. Plead guilty to the conspiracy, we'll dumb it down, you get off easy, being an ex-cop and all. Case closed, we all go on to other things. I'll leave your ghetto friends alone. They're young, they'll be around a lot longer than you so it would be heroic of you to do it for them, right?"

Carson suddenly stopped and waved his hand in front of his face. "You son of a bitch," he said, getting up out of the chair. He left the room, standing outside for a few minutes to let the air clear.

Tommy enjoyed the laughter he heard from behind the one-way glass on the wall. He smiled and waved to whomever was behind it.

Carson came back in and regained his seat. "Do it again, Borata, and you'll be sorry. I promise. Anyway, what about it? Do you want to cop a plea to save your young friends?"

"Bullshit, Carson. You want a big score for your promotion. You don't have anything on me, and you know it. That priest was hurting kids, good riddance. Get out and do some real work. There's plenty of bad guys out there. Unless you're afraid to get out on the street, picking on kids and old, sick men instead."

He had hit another soft spot and enjoyed seeing Carson begin to flush in anger.

"I'm out there every day, asshole. Unlike your kid, who sits on his fat ass behind his desk. Maybe I need to bring him out with me once in a while," he countered.

Tommy thought his tone was threatening. "You know he doesn't have experience on the street. Leave him alone, Carson. I'm warning you. He's not involved in any of this—he never hurt anyone."

"Maybe that's his problem. Can't get out from under daddy's wing and be his own man. Maybe you're responsible for his, ah, shall we say, effeminate side."

With that, Carson had won the battle of taunts. Tommy lost control and rose, grabbing the front lip of the desk and tipping it over toward his nemesis. Carson stood as well, grasping the desk and easily halting its progress.

Tommy, overcome with sudden dizziness and nausea, was forced to sit back down. He felt short of breath, and tried to speak but couldn't. He became terrified he was going to have another seizure.

"Pathetic," Carson said at Tommy's attempt. "Now, back to the business at hand. What say you, Tommy Borata? We have a deal?"

Tommy felt his nausea worsening. He thought of things to help bring it on. *Worms. Fried in olive oil, greasy fried worms, with sardines and vanilla ice cream...*

He leaned forward, and projectile vomited across the desk, the hot red bile shooting across its smooth surface, splattering over the folder of papers and spilling onto Carson's lap.

Carson jumped up. "Son of a bitch, you fucking asshole," he shouted, yanking the door open and running out.

Tommy stayed in the chair, satisfied and smiling, vomit still dripping from his chin. A few minutes later a young cop entered with cleaning supplies and mopped up the mess, staring warily at Tommy.

Carson returned a short while later, wearing a change of uniform from his locker. "You think that's funny, don't you, Borata?"

"We better wrap this up—if you think the gas was bad, I've had a lot of trouble with diarrhea lately," Tommy responded, smiling. "And I'm too sick to clean up after myself."

"Yeah, smart guy? I'm going to consider that assault on an officer. Let's try this. Stand up, Borata." Carson pulled a pair of cuffs from his belt.

Tommy complied, turning and placing his hands behind his back, wrists together. "You got no case, Carson. I'll have my lawyer on the horn and be out of here in an hour."

"Maybe. But it'll be a productive hour." Carson stood and grabbed Tommy by the chain in the center of the cuffs, shoving him roughly out the door and down the hall. "I have someone I'd like you to meet. Maybe he can convince you to be more open about your role in killing that priest."

He pushed Tommy at a fast clip into the detention area. It was empty, except for a man who was alone and raging in a cell at the end of the row. "This guy's a real winner, Borata," Carson said over the man's loud rantings. "Brought him in a little while ago. Very crazy— drunk and jacked up on PCP. Seeing as how we're pretty full here, I thought you guys should share a cell."

Tommy remained silent, strategizing and watching the man bounce around the cell as Carson unlocked the door. *Don't show fear; don't give him the pleasure.*

Carson quickly pulled the cell door open and shoved Tommy in. He closed it and stood back to watch, folding his arms over his chest and smiling.

Tommy backed into the corner as the man stopped and sized him up, like a zoo animal that had just had something foreign thrown into its cage. "What the fuck do you want?" he shouted at Tommy. "Get the fuck out!" He moved nearer, throwing punches wildly in the air, still too far away to make contact.

"Guess what, Randy," Carson said to him. "Remember how you said you hate cops and spit on me earlier when they brought you in? Well, your new buddy here is Sergeant Tommy Borata, lifelong cop."

The man's eyes widened. "Fucking cop!" he shouted, rushing at Tommy. He threw a punch at Tommy's head, and Tommy ducked to the side. The small movement took great effort, as the disease and treatment had atrophied his once-muscular body to the extent that it felt like it was petrifying. Each movement caused the nausea to surge exponentially, making it difficult to keep in check. Randy's fist smashed into the wall, and he howled in pain, shaking it.

Tommy assessed the damage based on the sound of the impact. *Concrete, so that's probably broken. Down to one hand.* The man came at him again, this time grabbing the front of Tommy's v-neck t-shirt and throwing him to the ground, ripping it down the front.

Tommy turtled and worked to kick off his shoes as Randy rained kicks onto his back from behind him. The force of the blows knocked the wind out of him, and he struggled to breathe. He pulled his depleted legs up into his chest as far as he could, for once thankful about his extreme weight loss. He began working his cuffed hands down over his butt, struggling to pull them over his feet to get his hands in front of him. *Thank God he's not a big guy, and drunk as hell.*

"Watch his hands, Randy. Watch his hands," Carson coached from outside the cell. "Don't let him get the cuffs around!"

The man was oblivious to the commands as he kicked wildly at Tommy's head. Stars burst and swam in a sea of momentary darkness, and Tommy vomited again. The cuffs tore at his wrists and hands as he struggled.

Just as Randy moved around to the front to try to kick him in the face and stomach, Tommy was able to pull his hands to the front. Randy swung his leg back to kick again and slipped in the vomit, spinning and crashing down onto the cell's metal cot face-down. Tommy struggled to his feet and pounced on the man, putting his cuffed hands over his head and tight around his neck.

The man gasped and retched.

Tommy turned his head toward Carson. "Open the fucking door and get me out of here, or you're going to have to explain why I was in here with this guy, and why he's dead."

Carson panicked and swung the door open. "Get the fuck off him." He pulled Tommy away from the prisoner and shoved him out of the cell, swinging the door shut. He looked back to make sure Randy was conscious and breathing. Then he pulled Tommy back down the hallway toward the exit at the end, unlocked the cuffs, and shoved him out the door and into the parking lot.

"Mark my words, Borata. You'll be sorry," he said before slamming the door closed.

17 DINNER AT HOME

THE BLINDS OF THE CONVERTED bedroom that served as Tommy's office were drawn, cocooning him in darkness. He struggled to get comfortable on the couch as nausea churned at his stomach. He tried to empty his mind of the thoughts that rushed through it like cars screaming through a subway tunnel.

Above all, he fought the urge to vomit, trying not to think about the plastic-lined trash can at the ready within arm's reach. He pulled his blankets tighter, not wanting to get up again to boost the thermostat. *I can't take being this sick much longer.*

He struggled to get to sleep. *Anything to escape this misery.* He wanted to be there for his son, to be functional, to make up for everything he had subjected him to throughout his life. He wanted this night to be perfect, and for Bobby to go away from it happy. *A little sleep, some more meds, and I'll be okay.*

Through the dim light, he could make out the pictures that outlined his life on the wall. He'd memorized them over the years he'd sat at the desk in this study. He reviewed pictures of himself as a tough young Marine in Vietnam. He scanned past framed commendations. *All for what?* He lingered on the photos of himself and his young son fishing, camping, hunting. *I don't like to kill things anymore*, Bobby had said one day, and it all stopped.

He went through the pictures of himself throughout his police career. Pictures of him and his wife at happy drunken occasions, in better times. He wished for the opportunity to go back to any of those places in time, to be a better father, a better husband, a better cop, a better person. To undo the mistakes, many of them made due to hateful prejudices and too much booze. He had come out of the Marine Corps an idealistic, determined, and disciplined young man, and he'd let all of that get away from him over the following years. *I knew better. I thought I was a big shot.*

A soft tap sounded at the door. "It's open," he said.

Margie opened it, allowing the light in the hallway to flood in. She stood in the doorway, bracing herself against the frame. "They'll be here soon. Just letting you know," she said.

"Okay. Listen, take it easy on the sauce today, huh? This is very important for our son."

"I already know that, Tommy. Please don't tell me what to do. I can have a few, it's a social occasion."

"Yeah," was all he offered. She backed away and closed the door. As it shut, it blew in the fragrances from the meal she was preparing, which immediately made his nausea worse. He fought it off, lying still, eyes closed, concentrating on nothing, breathing as shallowly as he could manage.

When he felt stable enough, he rose and turned the dimmer up, allowing enough light to illuminate the clothes in his closet. He selected khakis and a button-up dress shirt, then moved gingerly out of the room, trying not to breathe in more of the food smells than he had to. He made his way upstairs to the main bath.

He laid out his clothes, opened the medicine cabinet, and carefully arranged his toiletries on the counter. After undressing, he stood facing the mirror and was momentarily shocked by the image of himself. He looked prepared to play the role of the Ghost of Christmas Yet to Come. He found it surreal; as if his own elderly father had returned as he was just before his own death, and was standing there facing him as a warning.

He lived miserable, he died miserable. His mind flickered between the tanned, muscular body, rigid face and Marine flat-top that he'd always seen in that same mirror, and the pale sagging flesh, heavily lined face and stubbled remains of hair that he now saw. *Jesus, I'm fading away faster now.* For the first time, he realized and accepted that he was moving rapidly closer to his end.

He cranked the shower hotter than he would normally, to fight off the chills. Steam filled the bathroom, and he was thankful when the mirror fogged. He stepped carefully into the shower to avoid losing his balance and falling.

As he moved his hands over himself with a soaped washcloth, he became even more conscious of his diminished body mass and the chronic pain that lived in each remaining area, accompanied by the damage done by the prisoner's kicks. He stopped for a moment and let the hot water wash over him, trying to enjoy the moment of peace and pretend that none of what was happening to him was actually real. *Just a dream. A very bad dream.*

He turned off the water and reached to pull a towel from a hook on the wall. After drying, he stepped from the shower and wrapped it around his waist. He remembered when that same towel would barely make it, having just enough to tuck in and hold in place. Now there was plenty of slack.

The mirror was still fogged, so he turned on the fan and wiped off a space just large enough to shave. He opened a box of razor blades and chose one to replace the dull one in his old-fashioned safety razor. He held the blade between his fingers and examined it. *Such a small thing, but I could use it to solve all of my problems right now. I need to be here for Bobby, though. Not much longer.*

As he descended the stairs carefully, he heard voices and laughing. The rest and shower had made him feel better, and his spirits picked up. *My son is here. My boy.* He started to choke up and remembered the purpose of the dinner. Bracing himself, he promised to make it a success.

"How's everyone doing? What's all this racket in here?" he asked as he entered the living room.

Bobby and his guest rose immediately. "Dad, this is Mike. Mike, meet my dad."

Tommy sized the man up on his way to shake his hand. *Seems okay. You'd never guess. Firm grip. Reminds me of me. I guess it's the same— kids look for partners based on their parents.* "Nice to meet you, Mike."

"Good to meet you, sir. Thank you for your service in the Marines and as a police officer. I've heard a lot about you," he said, glancing toward Bobby.

"Yeah, I bet. Don't worry, none of that is true. Just an old persona. I'm a sheep in wolf's clothing, especially now."

"Don't buy it," Bobby said with a laugh.

"What do you do, Mike?" Tommy asked.

"I run an auto body and repair shop."

"Good, a man's work," Tommy responded, wondering if the comment was appropriate. *I'm still figuring out how this all works.*

Margie was in and out of the room, bringing in snacks and refreshing their drinks. Tommy watched her carefully to gauge her level of inebriation. The signs were there—a wobble in her step, a slight slur—despite her skill at concealing them. He started to worry.

When she disappeared for an unusually long period of time, and their glasses had gone empty, he grabbed them and decided to check on her. After looking in the kitchen, he moved over toward the side entrance to the garage. He pressed his ear to the door and could hear a low, muffled voice. Unable to make out the words, he yanked the door open.

~*~

Bobby looked over at Mike. They sat close to one another, but not too close. "I wonder if I should put my hand on your knee or something," he said.

"It's too much like I'm having my best friend over. I don't want the purpose of this to be lost on anyone."

"Oh Jesus," Mike responded. "Let's take it one step at a time. I'm good so far. They know what's going on, and they're just getting used to it. I don't want to set the General off."

"Yeah, makes sense. My Dad's sick, I can tell, but he's being a trooper. That's not normal for him. He's doing it for us. That alone means a lot to me. It means he's okay with us, and that's why we're here, dealing with this awkwardness."

"Your mom is nice, too."

"Listen, you know she's drunk, I know she's drunk, my dad knows she's drunk. She thinks that nobody knows, that's how it works around here—it's how we've always functioned. Family secrets, skeletons in the closet and all that. I'm sorry about it, but she's really okay other than that one problem."

"Don't sweat it. My dad drinks too. Same thing, he thinks none of us realize how much. We hear all of the excuses; he needs to relax, rough day at work, etcetera. Some world, huh? Everyone spends their lives stressed out, self-medicating, and working their ass off, for what in the end? A lot of unrealized dreams?"

"Not for us, Mike. We're gonna make ours real. Tonight is the first step."

~*~

She stood wedged in the far corner of the garage with her back to him, the cord from the extension phone above his workbench stretched taut. Her hand was over her mouth to quiet the conversation. She spun around and saw him, a shocked expression on her face. "Okay, Diane, I love you. Got to go, bye," she said as she rushed to replace the phone on its cradle.

"Tommy. I came in to get more beer out of the garage fridge. I was just calling to check in on Diane."

He tried to suppress his anger, not wanting its physical or emotional effects to ruin the dinner for his son. "You were, huh? Since when do you need to hide in the garage to call your sister? And I don't think I've ever heard you say you love her."

"No, it was her, check the phone logs," she said, grabbing several perspiring beer bottles from the workbench. "The boys need a refill, and I have to check on the food…" she said as she rushed by him.

He followed her out of the kitchen, and they took their places around the dining-room table. He kept an eye on her as she bustled about, clearly rattled from their altercation. She set a large casserole dish filled with lasagna on a hot pad in the center of the table. "Dig in everyone, family-style," she announced.

Tommy tried to dismiss what had happened and keep the mood upbeat. He contributed to their light conversation but became annoyed as Margie repeated herself often and began to slur more heavily. When she looked at him, he glanced toward her large glass of red wine meaningfully, hoping she would switch to something else, at least for the sake of their son.

He could sense that Bobby and his guest were uncomfortable, and caught them occasionally eyeing each other sideways. He picked at his food cautiously and soon noticed that everyone was done except for him. He'd only had the courage to sample a bit of bread and butter, and salad with mild dressing. He decided to try a bite of the lasagna.

As he chewed his first bite, he understood their discomfort. He resisted the urge to spit the food back onto his plate. Lifting the slice, he saw that the bottom was completely blackened, and the flavor of garlic was overpowering.

She saw him examining his food. "Bobby likes it crispy," she said.

"And with lots of garlic, too," Tommy replied, with a wink at his son and Mike. They laughed, and Margie got upset.

"You cook next time then, damn it!" she shouted to him. The tension in the room grew palpably as she got up and began clearing their places. As she took Mike's plate, she toppled his beer glass, spilling a river of foaming beer across the table and onto him. He jumped up, and Bobby rushed to clean it from his crotch with a napkin.

Margie watched her son's actions, looking appalled. "Fuck you, Tommy!" she said, grabbing her coat and car keys and heading out the door.

The revolt in Tommy's digestive system since swallowing the mouthful of lasagna was growing.

He knew he had little time left to get to the bathroom and wanted to clean the situation up as best he could. "Well, that went pretty well, didn't it?" he asked Mike and Bobby sarcastically.

"Don't worry, Mr. Borata," Mike answered. "My family's even worse. These things have a way of going wrong, the first time anyway until everyone gets to know each other enough to relax. I'm worried about her driving; should we go after her?" he asked.

"No," Bobby answered. "She's not going far, and she doesn't want us following her. This is status quo. Welcome to the Boratas'."

They began to clean up, working together. When Tommy could no longer stand the build up inside of him, he excused himself. "Hey, I'm sorry guys. Nature calls and all that, and these days, she's a fickle mistress. I'm going to be indisposed for a while. Mike, it was nice meeting you."

"No problem, Mr. Borata. I enjoyed the evening, and I'm sorry about the blow-up. Tell Mrs. Borata thank you for me."

They all shook hands, and Tommy hugged his son before making his way back upstairs to the bathroom. Each step became a challenge to make it before he exploded. He fought to avoid ending the night by embarrassing his son further.

Gasping and fighting his own body, clamping his rectum closed, he pushed open the bathroom door and worked at his belt furiously. He had just unfastened it and was trying to yank his pants and underwear down to get on the toilet when a torrent of explosive diarrhea let loose. He stumbled, his pants half down, and crashed onto the toilet.

"Everything okay up there?" he heard Bobby yell from downstairs.

He struggled to breathe, exhausted from the effort, his body still trying to purge itself. "All good, just a little slip. I'm fine, don't come up here, believe me!" he responded, kicking the door shut.

"Alright. We're heading out, Dad. Love you," he heard Bobby reply.

Holding his breath, he tried to remove his soaked clothing while still sitting on the toilet. He breathed in, and overcome by the stench, he felt the nausea grab hold of him. *So many enemies within me.* Launching himself from the toilet, he fell to his knees in front of the tub and yanked the shower curtains out of his way, stripping them from the pole. As he vomited into the tub, the plastic shower curtain rings rained down from above, onto his head and into the growing pool of vomit.

He stayed in the bathroom a long time, until the attacks were well over. The fan helped with the stench, but there was an awful mess to clean up. It brought him back to when Moses had had a similar attack, and he'd been there to help his friend through it, to clean him up and get him to bed. Depressed, he began to take care of the mess himself. *There's nobody here for me. No one to help. Nobody like that, anyway.*

~*~

Bobby and Mike walked out toward the car.

"Well, that went marvelously," Bobby said to Mike sarcastically.

"It just proved that your family is as screwed up as mine," Mike said, hugging him.

"Easy…neighbors," Bobby said, looking around nervously. Then he laughed. "Now look who's in a rush to get out of the closet."

"We're getting there. Like you said, tonight was a big step. I'm happy we did this."

"I'm happy it's over," Bobby answered. "I can't believe we just took that step, after dreaming about it for so long."

"You coming over for a while?"

"Yeah. I'd like to stay the night. I'm not sure I want to be around for whatever happens next here."

18 PRIVATE EYE

THE STENCH FROM THE DUMPSTER they were hiding behind was overwhelming.

Tommy took up a pair of binoculars as Molletier crouched next to him, peering through an identical pair. "You sure this is the right motel, and that's the right room?" Tommy asked. "You got this all scoped out?"

"I am a private detective," Molletier responded factually. "I am very good at what I do. Just watch." He paused. "You're sure you want to see this?" he added, with uncharacteristic empathy.

"It is what it is," Tommy said, doing his best to hide his emotions. "I have to know what I'm dealing with."

The sheer curtain in the first-floor room they were observing was slid three-quarters of the way across the window. They could only see the foot of the bed and a television on the dresser, which flickered with a mindless reality show.

The sound of an approaching car caught Tommy's attention. He looked through the binoculars across the darkened parking lot. As he adjusted the dials and the focus sharpened, he saw it at the far end, barely lit by the motel's neon sign. *Margie's fucking car.* The small hope he'd held that this was all some kind of coincidence was dashed.

He watched as she parked in a dark corner, then turned on the dome light and adjusted the rearview mirror to apply her makeup. She got out of the car and hurried across the lot, glancing around nervously.

For a moment, he wanted to pretend it wasn't her, that he was dreaming and he'd wake up any minute. He resisted the impulse to run to her and beg her not to do this. He wanted to convince himself she and his brother-in-law hadn't done anything yet, that it would be the first time, and thus everything would be easier to forgive—that they would cry together, profess their love, make everything right, and be happy together again for whatever time he had left.

Instead, he remained silent and held his position.

A few minutes later, there was movement in the room as a silhouetted figure rose from the bed, moved to the door, and opened it. A woman entered from the hall, still in shadow, and they became one. They briefly moved to the area of the window that wasn't obstructed by the curtain, and he could see them clearly through the binoculars. *My wife and my brother-in-law. I'll fucking kill you, Jack.* He could tell they were laughing and holding each other close. *I haven't seen her laugh in so long. I wonder if it sounds the same.*

"This is not easy," Molletier said. "You should go. Let me handle things. I can run the camera." He had swapped his binoculars for a camcorder, and Tommy could hear its gears whirring as the tape spun inside it.

"No," Tommy answered. "I can handle it." He returned to his binoculars, mesmerized by the scene inside the room. *They're leaving the light on. She never liked the light on when we did it. Maybe she was thinking about him then, in the dark with me.* They moved toward the bed, the area obscured by the curtain, and he watched as their shadows disrobed, leaving their naked silhouettes standing and facing each other for a moment, kissing before they both lay down on the bed. *She's lost weight. I hadn't noticed.* The television was switched to a pay-per-view pornographic movie. *She always said she hated that stuff.*

Then the ballet began, the two of them moving in unison, making love in various positions. He watched as the knot in his stomach became larger by the moment, as she rode above her lover, rocking. He watched as they switched and he mounted her, their lower legs and feet now visible at the foot of the bed, interlocking, and intertwining. The movement became more frenetic, and he saw his brother-in-law arch up and finish making love to his wife in a spastic conclusion. *Huh. One thing, he's got no stamina.*

He put the binoculars down. The eyepieces had fogged up, and he realized he was crying. His voice broke as he tried to speak. "Well, that sucked. I guess you were right. He ain't shit, Sensei." When he didn't get a response, he looked over to Molletier's position and saw that he was gone. He looked at the top of the dumpster and saw the camcorder, still whirring. *Oh, shit. Oh, no.* He stood, turned the camera off, and picked up his binoculars, refocusing on the room.

They were up now, and the silhouettes began to dress. He saw her shut herself in the bathroom. Then he saw Jack move toward the hotel room door. *Uh-oh. Here we go...*

As Jack reached for the knob and pulled the door open, another hand reached inside and flipped off the light switch. In the remaining glow from the television, he saw a flurry of movement. Two shadowed bodies flew around the room, while an orgy took place on the TV screen. Another shadow joined from the bathroom, and he could hear a woman's scream. A lamp went over, and then the television, and then the light came back on, and there was only one shadow—Margie, standing over what he presumed to be his brother-in-law lying on the carpet.

19 JOB OFFER

BOBBY SAT AT HIS DESK, trying to work while nervously checking the door to the station house. He could feel the effect of his anxiety and the several cups of coffee he had consumed on his heart rate. He spent the time wondering again why he was spending his life in a job he detested, around people he despised, only to please his father. *I'm going to quit. I just hope Dad's really okay with it.*

He heard a commotion outside and knew immediately that it was Carson and whatever follower he was partnered with that day. *Probably Jackson, as usual.* His stomach began to churn as he quickly retreated to the screen of his computer and the work he was supposed to be doing.

The door swung open, and his antagonist entered. "Good day, good day, you macho men and women in blue! I'm so proud to be part of a group of *macho* individuals such as yourselves. Make way for the biggest, baddest wolf in the den."Carson made his way through the room slowly, making sure all eyes were on him.

Bobby felt him coming closer and closer until finally, he sensed him standing there, looming over him as he pretended to concentrate on his work.

"Bobby, my boy. Don't you agree? A cop should be a macho, macho man, right? Not like that bunch of gay dudes in that stupid group that sang the song. Who was it, Village People? Right? Can't believe they had a gay guy dressed like a *cop* in that group. I mean, how do you do this job if you aren't a macho individual? The people expect it of us, right? They don't want a bunch of bozos for cops, do they, Bobby?"

Bobby felt his face burn. He knew that Carson was aware of his embarrassment and was enjoying it and that the entire station was watching him hold court. "Yeah, Carson.

Whatever you say. I'm kind of busy," he responded without looking.

His unease built as he waited to be outed in front of everyone he worked with, kicking off a long period of gossip and snickering behind his back. He wanted the floor to open up and swallow him, to be anywhere but there in that moment. It reminded him of when he was a kid: the waiting for inevitable, horrible things, and wishing for doors to open for him to escape through.

Carson leaned forward, sticking his head over Bobby's desk. "Listen, Bobby," he said in a whisper. "How'd you like to get out from behind that desk and do some real police work? Toughen up a bit. Make your old man proud of you, while you're still here."

Bobby processed the words, calculating them from every angle he could. He wondered if Carson was possibly sincere. *Maybe he thinks he can change me. I could make Dad proud, just once, before I quit. He'd be so happy to hear I was on the street, like him. Maybe I can get something on Carson, and get him to leave Dad alone.*

He decided he would do anything to escape the current situation, and turned to Carson. "You know what? I think I'll take you up on that." He said it loud enough for everyone to hear.

Carson stood up with a triumphant air. "Niiice," he said loudly. "Ladies and gents, this is what I'm talking about. Here's a man that wants to get out from behind the desk and do real police work." The others had grown weary of his show and were no longer paying attention.

He turned back to Bobby and spoke in a normal volume since he'd lost his audience. "Okay, so here's the deal. Jackson and I are going to stake out an abandoned warehouse on the South Side. There's drug trafficking going on there. You and I will observe from the upper floor; Jackson will enter from the ground on our signal, and we'll take them down. Hard."

Bobby's apprehension returned at the thought of being involved in something that dangerous. He tried to put on his best front and not let Carson know. "I'm in," he said, in a strong voice, the one his father had taught him.

"Excellent, m'boy," Carson said. "Full tactical gear. I imagine you haven't had yours on in some time. Better get it out and make sure it fits, if you know what I mean. Maybe trade up for a larger size if you need to."

"I've been through the training every year, Carson. Just like everyone else."

"Good, then. In a couple of days, you, Jackson, and I will go through the whole plan in the conference room, then we'll head out and scope the place out before we execute the plan and kick ass. Probably Monday—I'll let you know. Maybe there'll be a nice commendation or something in it for you. Have a nice weekend there, Boz—I mean, Bobby." He slapped Bobby on the back and smirked at him menacingly.

Bobby went about his work and Carson moved on, appearing to be satisfied.

Another officer came over and stood by Bobby's desk. "You sure you're okay with going on an operation with that idiot?" he asked Bobby.

Bobby looked up with frustration. "Why the fuck does everyone here think I can't do my job? That's *exactly* the reason I have to do it."

"Alright, alright. I wasn't saying that. I'm saying that I would be nervous myself going out with Carson. Something's wrong with that guy. Suit yourself, Bobby."

The officer walked away, and Bobby went back to his computer, pulling up the training manual on tactical operations to try to refresh his memory on the equipment and protocol.

20 BLUES JAM

TOMMY WATCHED AS LUCIUS and two other men moved around the far side of the dance floor at Wyla's Bar, rolling equipment out from a back room and running lengths of cable between microphones, amplifiers, and a mixing board.

Lucius came back behind the bar to give him a refill.

"What's going on? You having a band in here tonight or somethin'?" Tommy asked.

"Blues jam night," Lucius responded. "You play? Sing? There's a clipboard; put your name on the list, and the host will call you up for a set after we get started."

"I can belt out a little Springsteen."

"Nah. Nope. That white-boy rock star stuff ain't gonna work. Blues only, my man. Stevie Ray Vaughn might be okay."

Tommy checked his watch, glanced toward the door for his son, then continued watching the men set up. He wasn't looking forward to the hard conversation he and Bobby were going to have to have. In a way, he hoped his son wouldn't show, but he knew he'd have to confront the situation eventually. *Now is as good a time as ever.*

Bobby entered soon after, looking surprised and lost in the dive-bar atmosphere. He saw his father at the bar and joined him. "Damn, so this is where you spend your time. Is someone here, or is that for me?" he asked, motioning to the shot glass of whiskey on the bar in front of the empty spot.

"That's for Moses. You remember him, right? It's sort of a little tribute I do for him. I just leave it there. That was the stuff he liked. I miss that guy quite a bit."

A few musicians started to straggle in with their gear, and some milled around the impromptu stage and began warming up. The bar was filling with excited patrons taking seats at the tables.

Lucius came over and took Bobby's order after Tommy introduced them, pouring and delivering a tall beer. "So, what's up, Pop?"

Tommy hesitated and ran through his rehearsed talk once more in his mind before he began. "Listen, Bobby. There's something I have to tell you. Your mother and I..."

Bobby cut him off. "Oh, Jesus. That's it? Thank God. I was afraid you were going to give me bad news about your cancer."

"No, well, listen," Tommy tried to start again.

"Dad. I kind of knew. I mean, not for sure, but when things are going on in a house, the kids know, no matter what age they are. The parents may not want to admit it to themselves, but the kids always know. Even big kids like me."

Tommy remained silent, reflecting on Bobby's words, wondering how much he knew.

Bobby answered the silent question, at least in part. "I had a feeling that Mom had something going on. Little things, you know? Is that it, Dad?"

"Yeah," Tommy answered. "I guess so."

"I know it sucks, Dad. Especially with all you have going on right now. I love you both very much. I'm okay with whatever you guys are going to do about it. Just please, no fighting. If it's done, it's done. Mom told me she's sorry and she wants to work it out. Will you come back home? Have you talked to her?"

Tommy was relieved that he didn't have to spell it all out the way he'd planned. He'd been worried about his son's reaction. "I haven't talked to her. I just grabbed some stuff quick and left. I'm holed up in a shitty motel.

"To answer your question, Bobby, I just can't. I just don't feel it anymore. Obviously, your mom doesn't either. Relationships have a lifespan, and this one is done. I always believed that once one person crosses that bridge, is with someone else, there's no going back. I've never seen it work with others. It's been over for longer than I realized, I guess.

"We should've broke it off after the first time," he went on quickly. "We both made mistakes, you know that now. When it's done, it's done. I want to deal with this cancer now, and do my own thing with the time I have left. Your mother has a right to be happy, too. I'm gonna look around for a small place of my own, I think."

Bobby put his hand on his father's shoulder. "It's okay. Just please get along with her and support her. Actually, I'm looking around for a place too, but I'll have to hold off. I don't want her to be alone."

Tommy tried not to break down. "I guess the whole thing, that we were still the same little family living in that little house, was really just an illusion over these past years. It's all gone, what we had." He felt his son's hand squeeze his shoulder and realized that for the first time, their roles had reversed and his son was supporting him.

"It wasn't an illusion, Dad. It was love, and it's still there. It'll be there long after the house is gone. We love each other, that won't change. We had it, and we'll always have it."

"I love you, son," Tommy said, embracing him sideways from his stool. He was grateful that it had gone that well. "You think Mom will be okay there by herself eventually?"

Bobby laughed. "She ran the place anyways. We were just more work for her, and a pain in her ass. And you wonder why she drinks?"

Tommy laughed as well. The first set of musicians had been called up to the stage and were playing some upbeat blues. "I like this music."

"I always loved the blues," Bobby said. "It's the root and foundation of rock and roll and hip-hop. It gets a bad rap for being sad, but it's really a celebration of life, the good and the bad that comes along." He signaled to Lucius for another beer.

"Anything else you want to talk about, Dad?"

"Like what?"

"I don't know, well...the priest thing, any of that."

Tommy's demeanor changed. "Listen. Don't ever ask me about that. Ever. Okay?"

"Got it. Understood. I have more some good news, anyway, Dad."

"Go for it," Tommy said. "I could use some of that right now."

"I'm going on a detail with Carson tomorrow. There's a surveillance and takedown operation on some druggies on the south side at the old Turner warehouse."

Tommy became alarmed, recalling the conversation with Carson during his recent interview. "Bobby, please don't do it. Something sounds wrong there. It's not like Carson. I don't trust that motherfucker."

Bobby didn't mention the leverage that Carson had over him. "I think he just wants me to toughen up and be a 'real' cop. Maybe it's a peace offering, and this will get him off my back. He can be pretty brutal. You always said to get in some time on the street; that it was good for promotions on the admin side."

"Listen. You don't need that. You're good at what you do. You aren't used to this, Bobby. It's dangerous. We don't need more bad news."

"You don't think I can handle it?" Bobby's voice rose. "I'm trained. I do the training every year, just like every cop."

"Okay, settle down. If this is important to you, go for it. I'm just saying that you don't need to do anything to impress me, despite all the stupid stuff I said to you all those years. I'm proud of you just the way you are, son. You don't even need to be a cop if you don't like it. You had something else in mind, you told me once."

Bobby laughed. "Yeah, the dream I always dreamed. I'd like to be one of those guys by the beach who does the spray-can art for tourists. Maybe open an art studio by the beach."

"That sounds good, son. Keep me in mind if you need a partner. I can't paint for shit, but I'll run security and marketing, pass the tip jar. Life's too short. We all spend it busting our ass in jobs we hate, working for people we hate. We all gotta do what makes us happy." He took note of Bobby's empty mug and signaled to Lucius again.

Lucius brought the refill and asked, "You fellas want to sign up? You play at all, Bobby?"

"I can sing a few of the standards," he replied.

Tommy cocked his head back in surprise as Bobby put his name on the clipboard. "I never knew you could sing."

"It's something I do sometimes at the place I hang out. They have karaoke night. Plus, all my life, I've sung in the shower when you guys weren't home. I guess this is like karaoke, but with real music."

Lucius raised an eyebrow at him, a skeptical look on his face.

"I guess we'll see," Tommy said.

They talked for a while, Tommy enjoying what his guilt told him was something he should've started doing a long time ago—having man-to-man father and son time. Accepting his son for who he was had lifted a huge weight from him. It made him feel better, and optimistic about the time he had remaining. It was something he looked forward to doing a lot more. He found himself happier about the news that his son was finally going to find his own place than the other news, about him going on the street. *A long time ago, for so long, it would've been the other way around.*

They heard the jam leader call Bobby's name, and he rose from his barstool and went to the stage. "Break a leg, kid," Lucius called after him. Tommy swiveled on his barstool to watch.

Bobby and the musicians huddled for a moment, discussing the song and key, then took their positions. Bobby stood center stage, under a single red spotlight, as the opening notes of "Stormy Monday" filled the bar.

Tommy turned to Lucius, who stood watching from behind the bar with his arms folded. "Yeah, Allman Brothers," Tommy said to him.

"Shit, you mean Bobby Bland, white boy."

Tommy turned as his son began to sing the classic. He was amazed at what he was hearing. He wondered if it was just a father's bias until he saw the others seated at their tables with their mouths open, and the musicians on the stage smiling at each other and nodding their heads.

Bobby finished a stanza and nodded to the harp player, who stepped into the spotlight and executed a mournful but electrifying solo.

Tommy listened in rapt attention as his son belted out the song's lyrics, which covered the sadness and struggle of life, work, lost love, and faith. As Bobby finished and the room rose to a standing ovation, Tommy was filled with a pride he had sought his entire life—a pride he could never find in pushing his son to tackle sports and pursuits he was never suited for.

As Bobby made his way back to the bar, being congratulated by all he passed, Tommy embraced him in a bear hug. "Let's get outta here, kid. I'll give you a ride home. We'll get your car tomorrow."

They left and enjoyed the silence of the trip together. Occasionally, Tommy broke in to again describe how amazing the performance was, and how proud it made him. "You should take it up. You got something there," he repeatedly implored. "You could supplement the spray-paint art income."

As they pulled up to the house, Bobby asked, "You sure you don't want to come in?"

"I can't, Bobby. Besides, if she's home, she's probably drunk. Go on in and spend some time with her."

"One more question, Dad."

"What's that?"

"What the hell happened to Uncle Jack? He's all banged up. You have anything to do with that?"

"I don't know what you're talking about," Tommy answered. "And don't ask me again, please."

21 MOVING IN

THE REALTOR LOOKED AT TOMMY suspiciously. "You sure?" she asked. "I don't like going over there for showings."

"You don't need to," Tommy answered. "I know the neighborhood. I'm good with it."

"Oh. Okay then," she said, sounding surprised. "Let's wrap up the paperwork so you can focus on the move-in. I'll have a company I work with get in there, get the previous occupant's junk out and clean it up."

"I want it as-is. A friend lived there. The family is okay with it. Let's just sign the papers so I can get out of here."

Tommy sensed the woman's discomfort with him and was grateful for it, because it made her rush through the rest of the paperwork.

"So, Mr. Borata, will this be a one-year or two-year lease?"

"Just the one. I don't expect to be around much longer than that."

The statement only increased her speed, to Tommy's pleasure. They wrapped things up, and he departed, feeling the woman's stare as he left the office. A deadbolt clicked behind him.

When he reached the car, he looked at his image in the rearview mirror. The stubble he'd grown for the purse-snatcher operation was filling in to a short, full beard. He liked it, and felt it matched the transformation he felt himself undergoing. *Never had a beard before. Not regulation.*

He left the radio volume low on the way to his new dwelling. His mind tried to parse everything that had happened to him in the course of a short year. His comfortable prior life and body were fading away, and the treatment was slowly grinding his physical capabilities to a halt, despite the B-12 shots and drugs the doctor was trying and the various concoctions from the Korean pharmacy.

His thoughts drifted to Moses as he closed the distance to his late friend's old apartment. He reflected on their time together, good and bad. The laughs and struggles they had shared inside the decrepit old apartment. *Now that old cave will be my last stop, too. Maybe.*

His regret for involving Moses in his scheme returned to him. He pushed it away. *It's what he wanted, to go out big; to make a difference.* He thought about Molletier and asked himself if he was being fair to the man. He didn't want another friend to become a casualty. *He seems to enjoy it more than I do, though. Maybe a little too much.*

The Black Eagles were loitering around their bikes and sitting on the stoop as he pulled up to his new home. As he exited the Buick, they gave him a round of applause, and it brought his spirits up for the first time that day.

"There goes the neighborhood, brothers and sisters!" Lukas exclaimed. "Better sell now. Before you know it the block will be full of white people, bringing our property values down!"

They laughed, and he made the rounds, exchanging hugs, fist bumps, and soul handshakes with the group. "I guess I should get that Harley I've been thinking about," Tommy joked. "I used to ride, you know." He noted that Lukas still had deep bruises in several places on his face and head. "How're you healing up, kid?"

"I'm doing alright, almost good as new."

The Eagles got quiet and focused their attention on Lukas, their leader. "We have a little something for you, Tommy. In honor of your service to the 'hood; in honor of your friendship to Uncle Moses and us. Tass?"

The sole woman biker in the group opened up a saddlebag on her bike and extracted a black leather vest. She did a dramatic model pose and turned it to display the front and back. On the back, in arched yellow letters, it said "Black Eagles MC." On the front, above the left breast, a yellow nametag was sewn in. It said 'Tommy.'

Tommy rushed over to it as fast as his impaired legs would carry him, a smile burned onto his face. "Oh, damn," he said in genuine glee, trying it on. He looked at the group, then back down at the vest. "Are you sure? It's not a joke on the white guy?"

"Damn straight," Lukas responded. "Wear it well. Respect the code."

"First ever white member of the Black Eagles," Tass added.

"And hopefully the last," Gary said. Tommy wasn't sure if he was joking, picking up the only negative vibe in the group.

They gave him one more round of applause as he headed up the steps to his new apartment. "You want company?" Lukas asked.

Tommy turned. "Not quite yet. I got to settle in a bit and get my head around this. It's going to be tough. I don't even want to bring the bags up out of my trunk yet. I got to go up and commune with the spirit of Mos for a bit. I'm gonna smoke one and channel him into the room with me."

"Suit yourself," Lukas said. "I left a couple things up there for you, to help with the channeling and reminiscing."

Tommy went in and climbed the rickety staircase, then used his key, the one Moses had given him what seemed like so long ago, to open the door. He flipped on the light and stood in the doorway to take it in. The same ragged posters of Moses' musical heroes hung on the walls. His worn furniture was all in place. To the right was the bathroom, where he'd suffered in sickness as the disease had taken its toll on him.

There were pieces of paper on the coffee table, marking the evidence that had been seized by the police search after the priest had been executed. Tommy took those and threw them in the trash, leaving everything else in place. He seated himself on the old soft couch and closed his eyes.

He was startled by a sound and opened his eyes just in time to catch a small white dog that had run into the room and leaped into his lap. "Whitey!" Tommy said. *Moses' beloved dog.* "How are you, buddy? You miss your master as much as I do?" The dog licked Tommy's hands and nestled itself into his lap. He enjoyed the warmth and comfortable feeling of the dog resting there, and the feeling of being loved by the animal.

While the dog slept, he closed his eyes again and allowed himself to second-guess his choices. A part of him wanted to go back to his own home, to his wife and son. But that seemed like a part of another life, and the idea didn't sit well with him, like the thought of eating after a big meal. It was empty. *She let me down twice, and that's two times too many.*

He opened his eyes again, and something else caught his eye that shouldn't have been there—an old tin, sitting on the lower shelf of the coffee table, where it always had when Moses held court. *Damn.* He reached for it and popped it open. Inside were neatly rolled cellophane bags of marijuana, a few pre-rolled joints, and a lighter. *Moses' stash.*

He went to Moses' outdated stereo system and put on the Santana album they'd always enjoyed together, then came back to the couch and lit up, again closing his eyes to reminisce and reflect on the past, and consider his moves for the future.

After he'd finished the joint, he lay down on the couch and allowed himself to drift off to sleep. Whitey adjusted position to curl up against him.

22 DYSFUNCTION

THROUGHOUT THE FOLLOWING DAY, Tommy tidied up the apartment in anticipation of the visitor he was expecting that evening. With each small improvement, he weighed whether he was compromising the essence of his departed friend. Dusting was fine, he decided; removing the tattered posters was not.

He lit a few of Moses' candles and burned a stick of his jasmine incense. *It's not a date, asshole.* When he was satisfied, he sat on the couch and turned on the television just in time for the evening news. A knock came at the door, and he rose to check the peephole before opening it.

"Lukas, my man. What's up? Come on in."

Lukas entered and gestured to the leather vest proudly displayed on a hanger. "Nice to see you giving respect to those threads," he said.

"Damn straight. Now, where's my scoot?" Tommy asked, laughing.

"It's a BYOS kind of club, brother. We got enough trouble keeping our own running."

Whitey ran into the room to greet Lukas, who bent to pet him. "So what do you think? You want to adopt old Whitey here, or do some kind of shared custody? I'm always downstairs to help out. He doesn't like being in my place alone all day when I'm at work."

"Sounds like a winner," Tommy said. "I love this dog. I feel a little bit of Moses in him."

Tommy reached for the tin, and they began to share a joint as the news program droned on the TV. The presidential election campaign season was just beginning, and the focus was on a charismatic new primary candidate from the right.

"Republican Candidate Thomas Brand is firing up his base, promising jobs for the working class, and an economy invigorated by tax cuts for corporations and the wealthy," droned the newscaster.

"Damn," Lukas said. "Another rich old white guy promising salvation for the poor folk. Same old shit. They already tried all that trickle-down stuff. Nothing trickled down; all they did was hoard the profits, give each other big bonuses, and pass the rest on to the stockholders. Poor people ain't got no stock. And people ended up getting no raises and laid off anyway, same as always. Here we go again. Nothing changes with these motherfuckers. Same old song and dance."

They watched a clip of the candidate pompously preening before a braying audience.

"Look how fake," Tommy said. "What do you figure that haircut alone costs? This guy doesn't know anything about what it's like for other people. Born with a silver spoon from his rich daddy.

"And check it out, how many brothers and sisters you see in that audience? Nada. It's like 90% redneck white dudes."

Tommy sat back and gave him a pretend glare, the kind Moses would have given to him.

"Oh, shit. Present company excepted," Lukas laughed. "You know what I mean."

"You're right, though. Look at the audience, Lukas. Look what he's doing. They're all working-class. You hear any of this guy's spiel? It's veiled racism, homophobia, pandering to the religious right. Straight out of the Republican playbook, but *way* more extreme. This guy's dangerous. He's playing everyone."

"Yeah," Lukas responded. "He's dangerous unless you're a straight, rich, Christian white guy."

"Exactly," Tommy said, stabbing out the rest of the joint. "Hey, I got company coming, she's bringing me something to eat. You want to hang out? She's real nice."

"Oh-ho," Lukas said. "Date night?"

"Nah, just a friend, bringing me over some dinner, so I don't starve to death. I'm so nauseous though, I don't know if I can eat. I took extra meds, hopefully between that and the pot I'm okay."

"She must be a good friend, coming around this neighborhood at night. Anyway, I got to roll. Enjoy your time, Tommy. I'll check you tomorrow. C'mon Whitey, let's give the man some privacy."

Tommy saw him out, then retook his seat and continued watching the news. He was concerned that they might cover the murder of the priest again, so he switched the channel.

Hearing a car outside, he went to the window. He watched as a vehicle was expertly parallel parked against the curb and Carmen got out. Several of the Eagles were out front, and something was said to catch her attention. She laughed, obviously giving some of it back.

S*he's amazing.* He watched as she carried a stuffed grocery bag up the stairs to the building entrance. The male Eagles looked on with admiration as she passed.

He tried to breathe and relax as he heard her climb the stairs. The adrenaline and excitement were coursing through his body, something he hadn't felt in a long time. *It's not a date, stupid.* He rose to open the door so that she didn't have to knock.

She entered, and he nervously wondered how to greet her. His options were limited since she had her hands full, and as he took the bag from her, she reached over and kissed him on the cheek. "How's it going in the new digs, Tommy?" she asked. "For some reason, you seem to fit right in here. The bodyguards downstairs think quite highly of you, I can tell."

"Hello, Carmen. Yeah, it's okay here. Comfortable, you know? And cheap." They laughed as he took the bag to the kitchen.

Tommy went to the closet and retrieved the purse he and Molletier had rescued from the dumpster. "Hey, this look familiar?" he asked her.

Carmen turned and smiled at the sight of her purse. "Tommy! How did you get it back?" She rushed up to him, overjoyed, and gave him a prolonged kiss on the lips.

"A little old-fashioned police work, along with some strong coercion," he said. "I cleaned it up for you as best I could."

She opened it and withdrew some of her items. "My driver's license! I wasn't looking forward to the hassle of replacing that."

"Yeah, unfortunately, there's no credit cards, assuming you had some in there."

"I canceled them right away," Carmen said. She pulled a wad of bills from the purse and counted them. "Wait a minute…Tommy, I wasn't born yesterday. No way they left the cash in there. You did this."

"Hey, those guys are dumb," Tommy teased her.

"Yeah, and generous, too. I only took two hundred out of the bank, there's three here." She pushed the money at him.

"No, Carmen. You keep it. I can't stand to think about you getting robbed. I can take the hit, I'm in good shape. Keep it for the stuff you bought for dinner, and buy yourself something nice, like a .380 to keep in that purse," he laughed.

She peeled off a hundred dollars. "Take this or take it all. That's my final offer," she said firmly.

He didn't want risk upsetting her, so he took it. "You're a tough negotiator, I like that in a woman."

"Alright then," she said. "Here's the deal. You sit right down there and relax. I know you go back into treatment tomorrow, so you know the drill. I wanted you to have one big special meal before that ordeal. Just relax, let me do my magic here in the kitchen, and we'll have a nice meal together. It's taco night, you like tacos?"

"That sounds easy enough to me, and I love tacos," he responded, retreating to the couch. He tried to pretend to watch the TV, but he couldn't take his eyes from her, bustling around the kitchen. She seemed to know where everything was, and she hummed and sang softly to herself as she prepared the meal. She set the table for two and moved a few of the candles to it.

"I picked up some wine," Tommy said. "In case you want it. I don't partake myself."

She sat a wine glass at her place setting and came into the living room with a bottle. "Seriously? Mad Dog? Bum wine?" she asked him, holding out a bottle of Mogen David 20/20.

"Oh, shit, no," he answered, embarrassed. "I'm sure you know who that belonged to. Mine is on top of the fridge."

"Oh yeah," she said wistfully. "Good old Moses. I remember the first day you came in, you two going at it like cats and dogs."

"I'd like to go back," Tommy added. He cursed himself, wondering if he'd dampened the mood.

They ate, mostly silent other than the crackling of taco shells as they dove into the meal. "Are you sure it's okay?" she asked, as she refilled her wine glass.

"No, it's fine," Tommy responded. "I'm not an alcoholic or anything, as far as why I don't drink. It just wasn't doing me any good. I mean, in the cop days, it was excessive. Stress of the job, stress at home, and all that. I like the herb now, Moses turned me on. Much better."

"More wine for me," she said, and they both laughed again.

They finished and cleaned up, Tommy washing and Carmen drying the dishes. There was an awkward pause after they were done. He didn't know whether to invite her to stay longer and if he did, whether she would stay out of pity.

She saved him again. "So, what's on this ancient television. Maybe 'I Love Lucy'?"

"If it starts showing the news from the sixties, which is when I think it was built, I'm running out of here," Tommy said. He flipped the few channels that he could get reception for and found the beginning of *Casablanca*.

"I love this!" Carmen said joyfully. "Can we watch it?"

He tried his Bogart impression. "Of all the gin joints in all the towns in all the world, she walks into mine." She giggled, and he resisted the impulse to continue. "Sure thing," he said. "It's not like I'm a busy guy, and I have to confess, I do love the company."

"Well, I'm working the afternoon shift tomorrow, so I'm ready to relax," she said.

She brought over the wine bottle and her glass and set them on the coffee table, while he went to the linen closet and brought over more pillows for the couch.

"Oh, now this is comfy," she said, sinking back into it.

It was awkward sitting on the couch with the space between them, and he wished it weren't. She drained the last of the bottle halfway into the movie, and slowly, somehow, they closed the gap between each other. He could tell she was getting drowsier, and soon they were watching with her head on his shoulder and his arm around her.

And then they were both asleep, almost horizontal, lying back against the pillows on the couch. He roused, thinking it was a dream. He didn't want to move and take the chance that she would wake up and leave. Then she stirred slightly, her arm shifting to lie across his crotch. He wasn't sure whether he should move it; he certainly didn't want to.

He reached over and took her hand, leaving it there while the soft dialog and music of the movie played across the room. The candles burned and flickered, now mostly liquid in their glass containers.

She shifted again, and then turned and kissed him. He wasn't sure whether she was still half-asleep and dreaming and then wondered if it was just the alcohol. He kissed her back, softly, while trying to figure it out. It was something he could only dare to dream about during the short time he had known her. *The cancer times.*

Their kiss became prolonged and more passionate, as she released his hand and began to gently rub his crotch. He used his free hand to cup her breast over her delicate shirt. It had been a long time since he had experienced desire, particularly anything resembling this kind of true, raw passion. He wondered if this was okay, as she had been drinking. *Things are different today. And I'm still married.*

As they continued, he began to panic as he realized that despite his enjoyment and the excitement of what was happening, he was feeling no physical reaction. He could tell that she was becoming aware of the problem as well. She broke off their kiss, and his excitement turned to shame.

"I'm sorry," he said. "Damn Catholic guilt…"

They were sitting up now. "It's okay, Tommy. Listen, your body is under assault. Your mind is under tremendous stress. It's not unusual. I shouldn't have; I get a little crazy after that much wine. I should've taken it easy on the stuff. Wow, look at the time."

She started to collect her things, and he tried to talk faster to head her off, to get her to stay just a little while longer. "Hey, maybe you shouldn't drive. Stay here tonight. I'll sleep on the couch. You're right; I have a lot going on. You're beautiful, Carmen. This is something I've dreamed about…"

She smiled at him. "No worries, Tommy. Things are different these days. More casual. It's better that way. I gotta run, though. I had a wonderful evening."

"Maybe it's better if you remain just a fantasy to me, Carmen," he said sadly.

She kissed him, on the cheek again, and then left. He stood silently, looking at the closed door. His shame now mixed with anger. His face burned. He punched the wall, fortunately missing a stud, his fist sinking into the drywall. When he slumped back down on the couch, he could still smell her perfume, even as the sound of her car going down the road grew faint.

23 AIR-IN-LINE

TOMMY LAY BACK IN HIS RECLINER, the infusion console ticking away next to him. He was the only one in his pod, and the others were sparsely populated. Although a week had passed, he was nervous about facing Carmen after his disappointing night with her. Fortunately, she was away from the unit when he arrived, and Beulah had started his treatment.

Carmen arrived, and he watched them take a short break and chat with one another, laughing. He imagined them talking about him, his failure, and resisted the desire to rip the IV out of his arm and leave. *Easy, boy.* He felt like an awkward fifth-grader sitting next to the girl in school who'd refused him at a dance the night before.

He was startled by the warning beeps that suddenly came from his console. 'Air-in-line' flashed in red letters scrolling across the display. *Damn it.* Carmen noticed and broke away from Beulah, starting to head his way. He felt defenseless; he wanted to shrink into the chair and disappear. Carmen came over and repaired the problem in a businesslike manner.

She broke the tension by taking the empty recliner next to Tommy. "You busting up my equipment to get attention, mister?" she asked him with a smile.

"That equipment ain't all that's broken," he answered. She blushed, and he found it beautiful.

"Hey, anyway, how's it going?" she asked him, clearing her throat.

Tommy looked around. "Well, as you well know, based on our last get-together, not too groovy."

"Tommy—listen, don't beat yourself up. You're not a hundred percent. You're on a lot of meds. It's common."

He decided to assuage his embarrassment by changing the subject. "Where's everyone? No Molletier today?"

"He's on maintenance while he's in remission. Once-a-month treatments."

"What about the others who're usually here? Where's that creepy, annoying kid?"

She shifted uncomfortably, and he guessed the worst. "Business is slow," she answered. "I guess we're doing a good job here."

"Don't take too much credit. I think it's me. I get around people, and they go into remission. I think I'm sucking up the cancer from everyone else. I sure feel like I have mine and everyone else's in me. You're all looking for a cure; maybe I'm the cure. The cancer-vacuum."

She placed a hand on his knee and squeezed it. He was conscious that her hand fit easily around it. *That never would've been the case before.* He ignored the pain it caused him, unwilling to let her see it.

"You're going to be okay, Tommy. If anyone can beat this, it's you. Don't let the setbacks get you down. You have to be strong mentally. Stronger than the disease. Don't allow for a second that it's getting the best of you."

"Easier said than done," he responded. He looked at her, falling in love all over again. The way he had the first time he met her, in the very same spot. "Anyway, the stuff the doc has been giving me for those, um, unpleasant side effects has been working pretty well. I'm taking some B12 and some other stuff from Molletier, secrets from deepest, darkest Asia, to get my energy level back."

"Careful, Tommy—some of that stuff can interfere with your treatment."

"Well, whatever, it's working. I can get around better. Got a little more pep in my step, if you know what I mean. Listen, I have this amazing cannelloni recipe from my grandmother. Secret sauce and all that. What say you stop by and try some?"

She shifted in her seat and looked at the floor. "Tommy, I think you're an amazing, handsome, strong man. It's not because of what happened last time, but I shouldn't. You're a patient. I didn't come over that night intending for anything like that to happen. I drank too much, got drowsy, it happened spontaneously. I had no business letting it happen, I know better…"

"Yeah, I was there," he interrupted with an edge to his voice. "Or, more accurately, it didn't happen. But I've been reading up. They have something for that side effect too, right? You said I'm gonna beat it. If I had you, my will to survive would be a hundred times more. We could be good together, Carmen. I'm pretty well set. I'll get you the hell out of here, we'll go away to an island, live happily ever after…"

She removed her hand from his knee. "I care deeply for you. Don't make this difficult, please. I just can't, Tommy. I'm so sorry."

He looked at her and saw tears welling in her eyes. She stood and moved swiftly through the unit and out into the hallway toward the bathroom. He became angry at his situation, angry at his life and what it had been, angry at his fate. He switched on the television for his pod and tried to get his mind settled down. *Another bridge crossed and burned.*

He looked across the unit and saw Molletier coming toward him. "I thought it was your day off, Sensei? What're you doing here?" Tommy asked.

"Visiting a good friend. Sorry I am late."

"Oh, well, I don't want to hold you up then," Tommy joked. "Who's the lucky friend?"

That brought a rare smile to Molletier's face. He settled into the chair next to Tommy and began watching the television with him. Tommy appreciated his company and quiet demeanor.

The newscast began a story about the Republican primary candidate Thomas Brand. They showed the man giving a fiery speech to another raucous crowd waving Confederate and American flags. "They want us to accept their deviant lifestyle..." The crowd roared in approval. "They are an abomination, and the Bible says they are sinners..."

The crowd booed and began a loud chant. "No ho-mos. No ho-mos. No ho-mos." The candidate smiled at the effect of his words, at the measure of his influence on them.

"Next thing you know, they're gonna want to get *married*!" he yelled. The crowd went even more insane.

Tommy found himself enraged, thinking about his son and all he must have endured throughout his entire life. He considered his own former, regretful position on the issue. He remembered himself arguing in bars, drunk, that it was a *chosen lifestyle*. He considered his son, now with a clear and unprejudiced mind. *He was always that way. Born that way. His mom and I refused to accept it, blinded ourselves to it, and he worked to hide it his entire life. The hell he must have put up with in school, and nobody was there for him at home.*

The thought saddened him. He turned his attention back to what the candidate was saying. Anger overtook him once more, watching the ignorant, hateful people and the pompous narcissist manipulating them.

He didn't realize he had balled his fist and cocked it back, ready to take out the screen, until Molletier's hand flew out to grab his wrist. "Television costs money. Breaking it helps nothing," he said.

"Makes me feel better, though," Tommy responded, relaxing and dropping his arm back by his side. He switched the set off. "I'd feel better putting a bullet through that guy's head."

"Not to worry. He's not going to go far. Not in this country. Many naive people, but also many, many people smarter than that."

"We better hope so. I'm gonna get some sleep, Sensei, okay?"

"Sleep. Body heals during sleep. Wake, and I will be here."

Tommy closed his eyes. He thought of when Moses had gotten much worse, and he was in remission himself—how he'd come by for Moses' treatment for moral support. Now the roles had been reversed, with him in Moses' unfortunate place, and Molletier in his. *Not good for me.*

24 STAKEOUT

CARSON SWEPT THE FLOOR of the abandoned warehouse with his flashlight. When the beam hit what he was looking for, he walked over to the spot. "You sure this will hold, Jackson? He's got to weigh at least two-fifty."

"It's an old queen-size mattress I found at the dump, and a queen blow-up camping mattress I had in the garage. Should do the trick." Jackson leaped onto the stack for emphasis.

"Queen-size, how appropriate," Carson commented. He looked at the ceiling, shining his light on the old beams and plywood. The sheet of plywood directly above the mattresses had a freshly cut groove running end to end through the center.

"You sure about this? If anything goes wrong and the chief finds out he's going to go fucking crazy. What if he gets hurt?"

"Nobody is going to get hurt. He'll be geared up. After he shits his pants and we get done laughing, we'll just say that it's a rite of initiation and everyone's done it." He put his boot on the mattresses and pushed down. "This is more than enough. Just make sure you're rolling with the video camera.

"I just want to put a little scare in him. We don't need any flaming queers in the station. It's a risk to *our* safety. We'll tell him he needs to respect the blue wall of silence, or else. The video is going to be hilarious. I can't wait to see the look on his face. Make sure you get him coming through the ceiling."

"Where's he at?" Jackson asked.

"He's down the block, in the unmarked car. I told him to sit tight while I scope things out here."

"Alright. Let's do this and get the hell out of here."

Carson switched off his flashlight and headed back to the car. As he approached, he saw Borata sitting nervously in the passenger seat, a tactical helmet cocked awkwardly on his head. *What a pathetic homo.*

He reached the car and rapped twice on the hood, startling the occupant. "Let's do this, Bobby-boy." He watched as Borata struggled from the vehicle in the bulky gear, sweat already pouring from his face. "It's time. With me," he commanded.

Carson moved quickly down the street in a crouch, knowing that Bobby would have trouble keeping up. He could hear the out-of-shape man behind him begin to struggle with his breathing, and his poorly secured and ill-fitting gear jangled. *Thank God this isn't real. We'd be dead already. Moron.*

They reached the warehouse, and he led Bobby up a narrow side staircase to the second floor of the building. He twisted to check on his partner's progress and saw him struggling, well behind. "Let's fucking go, fat-ass," he said in a hoarse whisper.

"I'm trying," came the reply from below.

They gained entrance to the darkened upper floor. Carson shone his flashlight as Bobby tried to catch his breath. He whispered again, "Okay, Borata. Here's the deal. Head over to the other side, quietly. Take up the position over there, so we have both ends of this floor covered. When you get to the other side, you'll find a hole in the floor where you can watch what's going on. We'll wait for the bad guys to show up. Watch for my signal."

Carson became aggravated as Bobby silently listened, nodding his sweaty face up and down the entire time, clearly terrified, still out of breath. "You need to get in better shape, Borata. Jesus."

He felt a tingle of anticipation and excitement in his groin as Bobby started to make his way to the other side of the floor. It was a feeling he'd known as far back as he could remember: heading into the woods to check his traps, sighting a deer through his scope and getting ready to pull the trigger, cornering some loser in the boy's bathroom of his elementary school for lunch money, about to blindside someone on the football field.

The wood began to creak as the heavy man duck-walked across it, stopping to steady himself and fumbling with his own flashlight. Carson suppressed a laugh at the sight. *I should be filming this part too.* The sounds became louder as Bobby made it almost halfway, just short of where the compromised sheet of plywood waited.

Bobby stopped and turned back to Carson. "I don't know. I'm not sure about this. I want to go back. This isn't for me."

"Move it, fatso, before you blow our cover!" Carson hissed at him. *So close, don't chicken out now.*

Bobby took another couple of steps forward, and there was an almost inaudible squeak of dry wood. He took another step, and the same sound came forth—a bit louder this time. He was almost to the center of the sheet. He took a third step, and the wood began to groan. Bobby stood, and realizing the danger, took a half-step back toward safety, but it was too late.

"Carson, help me…" was all he was able to say before the compromised plywood gave way. He stepped to the side to try to reach firmer footing and reached out for the crossbeam, and in the instant the board snapped in half, he looked at Carson, terrified.

Carson looked on, smiling in the moment it took for Bobby to disappear through the floor. In his struggle to get to safety, Bobby had lost his balance, swinging his body in an arc, and on the way down his head struck the beam with a sickening sound, the tactical helmet flying off. He disappeared. There was a loud pop and a sickening thud, and Jackson's laughter from below suddenly stopped.

Carson rushed over to the new hole and looked down. Bobby was sprawled on the floor, his lower half laying on the deflated air mattress and his upper half on the concrete. Blood was starting to pool around his head. The half-sheets of plywood lay on either side of him. Jackson stood in shock, the camera at his feet. "We got to call an ambulance," he said. He then bent down and started to work through the emergency medical protocol, checking for breathing and a pulse.

"Fuck that. He'll be okay. Let me come down and check him out."

"He's breathing, for now. Fuck you, Carson. I'm calling it in. Start thinking about how we're going to explain this."

"I'm going with a training exercise gone wrong. Call it in. I'll start working the scene to match our story."

2 THE WOLF

THE LAST CHEMO SESSION hit Tommy harder than any other—far harder. He wondered if recent events had contributed to that. His spirits were lower than he could remember.

For the first time, he found himself unable to drive himself home. Molletier took the wheel, and Tommy offered to pay for his taxi home. As they reached the car, Molletier helped him in, and once they were both inside had to help him fasten his seatbelt. They exited the hospital, rounding a curve at high speed and tossing Tommy against his door.

"Jesus, Sensei. Take it easy or I'll be spewing puke all over us."

"Sorry," Molletier responded.

They continued to the main road, with Molletier still driving at a speed uncomfortable to Tommy. Watching the street signs whiz by increased his nausea, so he closed his eyes and tried to relax. *He's a good friend, doing this for me.*

He drifted away in what felt like seconds, and dreams took him over. He welcomed them, welcomed the escape from his reality.

The woods were dense, and he and Bobby pushed through thickets together. Tommy was wearing standard hunting camo, but Bobby had his rumpled police uniform on. They both carried shotguns and tried to move with stealth. They whispered things to each other, but strangely Tommy couldn't understand Bobby's words.

"It's like the old days, right, son?" he asked.

"A man's son is his best friend. You're everything to me, Bobby. You're a good man, that's what makes me proud. It's all a man can ask, right? For his kids to become responsible adults."

Bobby was saying something, trying to tell him something, but he couldn't hear it. Tommy sensed some urgency to what Bobby was trying to communicate. His conscious mind fought with the dream representation of himself to ask his son to speak louder, but the dream-self either wasn't listening or couldn't act.

Bobby grabbed his shoulder and motioned for him to wait, then moved ahead on his own, silently, slowly. He scanned the woods ahead as if he had heard something.

Danger. Something bad's about to happen. He tried to call Bobby back, but this time he found himself muted: he was trying to scream to his son, but no sound would come from his open mouth.

He looked beyond his son's position and saw the brush parting—something unknown was coming at Bobby at a fast pace. He heard a growing snarl. He tried to rush to his son, still trying to warn him, but his feet were cemented in place. He pulled at them, tugging at his pants leg to release himself as a massive wolf appeared just ahead, on a beeline for Bobby. He raised his shotgun and sighted.

"Bobby, Bobby!" he dream-shouted, but the words wouldn't come out, even as he sighted down the barrel of the long gun. Bobby stood still, seeming to hear the wolf but looking in the wrong direction for it. Tommy tracked the wolf through his sights and as it bore down on his son, white teeth bared and eyes blazing.

His eyes were clouding now, and he felt hot tears making rivers down his cheeks. He pulled both triggers to unload the dual barrels of shot, hoping his son was still too far to the side to get hit. There was nothing—the gun wasn't loaded. He screamed and continued pulling the triggers as he watched the wolf launch itself upward at his son's neck and then take him down to the leaf-strewn forest bed.

Car horns blared, startling him out of the dream. He woke screaming and looked up to see them flying through a red light, with cars entering the intersection from both sides and screeching to tread-burning halts. Aggravated drivers in those cars were yelling silently and giving them the middle finger.

He looked over at Molletier, who was driving with his hands at the ten and two position on the wheel, relaxed as if nothing were happening.

"What the fuck was that? You went through a red light, Sensei. I'd like to die from the cancer, sometime in the future, not getting t-boned by a pickup truck." He grabbed his stomach and fought to hold down the bile that was trying to escape, gulping to stave it off.

Molletier turned sideways to look at him. "Sorry. Out of practice. Lost license years ago. Just trying to help."

"Lord have mercy," Tommy answered. He was about to ask to switch but recognized that they were only a few blocks away. "Okay, slow it down, we're almost there."

They pulled up in front of the apartment, and he was disappointed when he realized that the Eagles were all at work. He'd lost track of weekends and weekdays. *At least this guy doesn't have to try to parallel park.*

Molletier helped him upstairs and into the bathroom, and when Tommy had finished the sensei sat him on the bed. He removed Tommy's shoes and turned the bed down, then helped him in. "You want me to prepare herbal soup?" he asked Tommy.

"Thanks, Sensei, but I can't eat anything. I'd toss it right up. I just gotta get some sleep. I really appreciate your help. Sorry I got a little cranky about the driving. The phone's in the living room; you can call a cab." Molletier refused his offer of cash and closed the bedroom door as he left.

Tommy slept through the afternoon and into the evening. He woke, stirring in the darkness, and heard the sound of a car pulling up outside, and then the door slamming. He rushed to the window, hoping that Carmen had returned, his heart beating quickly.

In his rush, he stubbed his big toe on the coffee table and cursed. Reaching the window, his hopes were dashed. There was a squad car on the street below.

He waited as the heavy footsteps came up the stairs toward his door. *This can't be good. Better not be that asshole Carson coming to hassle me.* He opened the door as soon as the knock sounded, and found Chief Patterson standing there.

"Roger, come in, come in. What's up? Kind of late for…"

Patterson interrupted. "Tommy, we've been trying to figure out how to reach you. Margie said she had no idea where you were. It's

Bobby—he's had an accident. Let's get to the hospital."

26 COMATOSE

THE BEEPING AND THE GLOW of the medical equipment was all too familiar to Tommy, but not from this perspective. He sat next to his son's hospital bed, holding his unresponsive hand. Bobby was almost unrecognizable—what was visible of his head between the bandages was swollen, discolored, and bloated.

Tommy made no attempt to wipe away the tears that streamed down his face. Guiltily, he ran through the scenes and events of his son's life again, damning himself for many of them. When he got to the present, he allowed himself a small reprieve due to his acceptance of who his son really was, and their new bond.

He turned his thoughts to hope for the future, that Bobby might have a future, and how he would make sure that his son would do what made him happy and never have to wear a badge again. Then he changed his thoughts to what really made him feel better—how to make Carson pay.

The door opened. Chief Patterson entered and took a seat. "How's he doing? Any change?" he asked.

"No. They've stabilized him for now. Traumatic brain injury; lots of swelling. They may have to operate to take the pressure off if they can't stop the swelling.

"Roger, I want to know what the fuck happened to my kid. In *your* squad. On *your* watch."

"Tommy, we've been friends a long time. I've known Bobby since he was a little kid. I'm shook up seeing him like this, too. Trust me, I'll get to the bottom of this, I'm on it. I love that kid. Investigating this is the highest priority I have, believe me. Carson is suspended without pay. I have my best people on this, and they're no fans of that asshole."

"I'm a sick guy, Roger. I got nothing to lose, not a lot of time left…"

"Exactly what I thought you'd say, and what I was hoping you wouldn't say. Tommy, *please* don't take the law into your own hands. You can't help Bobby if you get locked up. You'll have no future with your son, other than on a phone between a very thick piece of glass in the joint. Let me handle this. Trust me, he'll pay."

Tommy shifted in his seat and looked out the window, past the rain streaming down the panes of glass, to the bleak sky and landscape beyond it. "I'm gonna try to stay out of it, Roger. But I'll tell you this, I ain't gonna wait long. Look at my boy here. Look at my beautiful baby boy. We were just getting to know each other, finally."

"Give me time. You staying here tonight? Margie's been in?"

"I'm staying. She was here, she's a mess. I sent her home to sleep in her own bed. She's probably sitting at the kitchen table right now with a bottle of scotch. Or somewhere else."

Patterson rose and gripped Tommy by the shoulder. "Hang in there. I have work to do."

"Turn off the light on your way out, please," Tommy asked.

He left, and Tommy positioned an extra chair to face his, forming a makeshift bed. He fluffed the pillow he'd been given by the nursing staff and threw the blanket over himself. He lay on his side, facing Bobby, alternating in the dark between grief and rage.

His cop's instinct alerted him to the presence of another person, bringing him immediately out of his slumber. He sat up and tried to focus on the shadow that stood over Bobby. "Who are you?" he asked. "What do you want?"

The man came closer and put out his hand. "It's Mike, Mr. Borata."

Tommy saw that he was crying. He pushed the extra chair away and sat up. Mike leaned in to embrace him.

"Here, sit down, please," Tommy said. He brought Mike up to date on Bobby's status and what he knew about what had happened, which was little more than that there'd been an accident on the job.

"Listen, they're keeping me in the dark about the details on this, afraid I'll do something,"

Tommy said. "Is there anything you might know?" He didn't want to prejudice the man with his own suspicions.

He sensed Mike's discomfort, and added, "Look, you two were together. I get it. I'm okay with that. We had a nice dinner…well, sort of. I just want to get him better, and to figure out what happened. Work with me and tell me anything you might know. Anything Bobby might not have shared with me."

Mike thought for a minute and began slowly. "We were in a club not long ago. It was a gay club. We were having a fun night, but then some big guy came in dressed like a cowboy. Bobby saw him, said he knew the guy and that he was trouble. Said the guy was a cop, from the precinct.

"What'd he look like?" Tommy asked, wanting to be sure.

"Big. It was costume night, so he had big sunglasses, a hat, and fake mustache on. Big guy, though. Anyway, Bobby saw him coming and went to the bathroom. The guy hassled me, said he was looking for someone. Then he went into the bathroom and came out after a minute. He left, then Bobby came out and said he was sick and wanted to leave."

"Did he say what happened in there?" Tommy asked.

"Yeah, he said the guy was a cop from his station house who had been bothering him. The weird thing was that the guy was coming off like he was some anti-gay hardass, but I was watching him in that club, and the way he talked to me, I think he was into it. He seemed to be interested in me, and what was happening in there."

Tommy took a moment to process everything he'd heard before he spoke. "I need you to do something for me, Mike. If the cops find out about you and question you, don't tell them about that. And, never, ever tell anyone that you told me any of this. Understood? Can you do that, for Bobby?"

Mike looked over at Bobby. "I understand. You can trust me. I just want him to get better. I miss him. I'll do anything for him. Including taking out that son of a bitch that hurt him, if he had anything to do with it. Sounds like he did, from how you're reacting."

"Alright, then. You mind keeping watch here while I go to the cafeteria for some grub?"

"No, of course not. I'd like some time alone with him. I got things to say, even if he can't hear me."

Tommy left and took the elevator down to the hospital cafeteria. He filled his tray with food but was too sick and distraught to eat. After dumping it into the trash, he poured himself a large Styrofoam cup of black coffee.

After paying at the register, he walked to the farthest point he could find, to be able to sit alone. As he sipped his coffee, staring at the wall, he heard a voice behind him.

"Mind if I join you?" Carmen asked.

"Sure," he responded.

"I went up to the room and was told you were here. I heard about Bobby. I'm so sorry, Tommy."

"He'll be okay. He's a tough kid."

"It's pretty serious. We always have to hold out hope and be positive. But I have to tell you, Tommy, he's hurt pretty badly."

He slammed his fist on the table. "I *said* he's going to be okay!" He looked at her and fought off the memory of the shame and embarrassment of their night together and her subsequent rejection of him at the chemo session. He wasn't attracted to her anymore, and he didn't want to be around her. He found that he resented her presence, something he never would've thought possible.

She looked at him, and he could sense her gauging him. Tears started to form in her eyes. She got up, kissed him on the cheek, and left without saying a word.

27 DATE NIGHT

UNABLE TO FIND A CLEAR SPOT on the coffee table filled with stacks of money, Jackson placed his drink on the floor.

"Careful," Carson said. "This carpet cost me a mint. Had everything replaced when I moved in."

"And you had to go with pure white, of course. Don't you worry?" Jackson asked. "You're a city cop who drives a Porsche 911 and lives in a luxury condo. Don't you think that looks a bit suspicious?"

"Well, I don't have friends, and you're the only cop that's been here. If it comes down to it, inheritance and lots of overtime, that's my story," Carson said, laughing. "I'm sticking to it, and you are too, right?" The smile left his face as he waited for Jackson's answer.

"I'm in this as deep as you are, so there's no problem there. Let's get this counted up so I can get the hell out of here. Besides, this Borata thing is much more likely to take us down than any of this. That was a major fuck-up, Carson. I'm worried."

"It'll be fine. Just keep your mouth shut and stick with the story. We were trying to help him, trying to help him gain respect for himself, from his old man, and around the station. He insisted on taking the lead. We had no way to know the plywood was faulty. It could've happened to either of us. The mattresses were there from the bums that use the place to crash. You straight on all that?"

"Yeah, sure. We still have to worry about his crazy-ass old man coming at us."

"That fucker's too sick to get out of his own way. You see what he looks like now?" Carson began cleaning up the table. "Okay, you do need to get the hell out of here. I have a date coming, and I have to put all this away and take a shower."

Carson grabbed a handful of the stacks of bills and held them to his chest. "I love it. We earned this. We put our lives on the line every day, right?"

"Whatever you say," Jackson answered. "I'm only in this to put my kids in a better school and retire early. I'm getting nervous."

Carson stopped what he was doing and stared at his partner. "We just talked about this. You getting nervous makes me nervous. You're not getting any funny ideas, are you?"

"Of course not. If one of us goes down, we both go down. You know that, it's our deal. Do we have to be into everything, though? It's getting too big. It was one thing when we agreed to tip the dealers and hookers off that there was going to be raids. But now we're directly involved with their business. It's risky. I don't want to get too greedy; this isn't what we talked about in the beginning."

Carson thought about it for a moment. "I get a little worried sometimes too. Too many do-gooders around the station. I'm off the job for a while anyway, so I'm sure they're watching me. Maybe we should dial it down for a while. I was gonna back off anyway when I get my promotion and start making better cash. Maybe we should start wrapping it up now. Quit while we're ahead, especially with the attention this Borata thing is bringing."

"You're running the show, Carson. If you want to do that, I'm okay with it."

Jackson left, and Carson stood at the window, looking down over the lights of his city. *Fuck that. Maybe I'll just cut Jackson out. Why should I quit? I have cover from up the ranks, as long as I provide a cut. I could run this whole fucking deal if I wanted to. Who's going to stop me?* He went to the bar, poured a large glass of whiskey from a crystal decanter, and drank half of it down.

He put the stacks of cash away carefully in the safe he had hidden in his bedroom's walk-in closet, and then showered and dressed for the visitor he was expecting.

He used the remote control to start his favorite psychobilly country music mix, dimmed the lights, then lay back on the leather couch and closed his eyes.

The door made only a slight noise as it opened, and a tall, muscular black woman with an oversized afro moved stealthily into the apartment. The music blared as Carson slept sitting up on the sofa, his back to her. The woman opened her purse and extracted a pair of pantyhose, positioning herself carefully behind him. She paused as a song ended, waiting for the next to begin.

A thrashing of guitars, drums, and banjos began, and she continued toward her target. When she was within reach, she pulled the ends of the pantyhose tight between her fists, looped it over Carson's neck, and twisted it tightly.

He tried to escape, tugging at the hose around his neck. Realizing it would do no good, he reached back and grabbed her arms, pulling her over him and onto the couch. The larger woman landed on top of him, taking the advantage by pinning him down with her weight. She continued to hold the ligature firmly until he started to gasp, and then she loosened it slightly.

She reached down and yanked up the skirt he wore, then yanked down his pantyhose. He stopped struggling, semi-conscious, as she let go and reached for her purse, removing a tube of lubricant as he paused for a moment to wait. It was the one part of the fantasy that he still wasn't comfortable with. She entered him from behind and rode him until they were both spent.

Carson sat up, his face still shades of purple and red, coughing and trying to catch his breath. She sat next to him, replacing her wig and heels. "Did I do alright, Detective Carson?" she asked. "Like you said?"

He reached over and slapped her hard across the face. "I fucking told you, call me Susan when I'm in character!" He slapped her again. "Do you fucking understand, faggot? Now get your black ass out of here. Get it right next time, or you're done."

"You gonna tip or anything?" she asked sheepishly.

He cocked his fist back, and she backed away until she was at the door, and went out as quickly as she could.

28 TRIALS

THE CAR AHEAD OF HIM CREPT slowly into the parking lot. Tommy could see just the top of the woman's head of pure white hair, and the blue handicapped parking tag hanging from her rearview mirror.

"C'mon, little old lady, let's go," he said to himself. *In the old days, I'd be laying on the horn heavy by now.* He took pride in the fact that he was being patient, and took pity that at her advanced age, she had no one else to drive her to the hospital. *And not much money, judging by her car.*

They approached the handicapped parking, and she put her blinker on to signal her intent to take the last remaining spot. He took note that only half of the vehicles occupying the other spaces had the appropriate designation to use them. As she slowly moved toward the space, a sports car approached quickly from the other direction and flew into the spot. The woman kept looking.

A man jumped out of the sports car in a jogging suit, his sunglasses propped on top of his head. Tommy rolled his window down. "Hey, what the fuck is wrong with you?" he asked the man, as he walked by at a fast clip. "You don't look too handicapped to me, pal."

The man turned toward him. "Just running in quick to pick up a prescription, sorry dude," he said, moving even faster toward the entrance.

Tommy resisted the urge to get out and confront the man. *I got no juice now. He'd put me down fast, then probably sue me. Looked like a damn lawyer.* He pulled into a spot farther down the row and popped his trunk. Opening a large toolkit, he selected a pair of heavy-gauge nails from a tray of assorted fasteners.

As he passed the man's vehicle, he knelt down and angled a nail from the blacktop into the front and back of a rear tire, ensuring at least one would find its target whether the man pulled forward or backward. Satisfied, he entered the hospital.

Tommy looked around at the items in the exam room: plastic representations of body parts, both normal and diseased. Pictures on the wall of the same. All were painted in gay, bright colors. He remembered being in the doctor's office as a little kid, intimidated and afraid of the same pictures, sculptures, and the seemingly medieval instruments of pain and torture lying on trays.

He moved to the window and saw the sports car sitting at a tilt near the parking lot exit. The man in the track suit was circling it, gesturing animatedly while talking into his cell phone. He watched as the old woman's car moved slowly by and pulled into the street. *Karma's a bitch*, Tommy thought, and then erupted in laughter at the sight.

The office door opened, and Doctor Mason entered. "What's so funny, Borata? It's good you still have your sense of humor. It helps to fight the disease."

"Just people," Tommy said. "Stupid people." He sat back down on one of the plastic chairs.

Doctor Mason scanned his charts, then put them away and sat down next to Tommy, now wearing a serious expression. "Alright. To be honest, the trials did well for you. Your body reacts well to them…it's been a good run. The scans have been pretty clear, or at least we've been able to stabilize some of your lesions and tumors so that they don't grow. The ones in your brain that we've been zapping are also clear."

Tommy asked a series of rapid-fire questions. "What about after this trial is done? You said it's *been* a good run. It'll run out of juice like the others, right? Didn't you say it would only work for a while, until the cancer figures out a way around it? What about the last trial drug you mentioned, the Forbaxatel? That one's the holy grail, right? Any news on my mutation results?"

The doctor cleared his throat. "Which gets me to my point. I said that the scans *have* been pretty clear, but now we're starting to see some progression. I'm sorry, Tommy, but you didn't test positive for the mutation we'd hoped for, the one you need to get into the Forbaxatel trial."

"Which means what? The rocks you talked about, crossing the river and all that—I'm out of rocks? Stuck in the middle of the rising river, going to drown?"

"Our job is to keep you going until the next one. There's always more coming out of the research labs."

He began to feel desperate. *Bobby might need help, I may need to care for him for a long time.* "Doc, you said I've reacted well to other trials. C'mon, let's take a shot at this Forbaxatel one. What do I have to lose, right?"

"It's not my decision, Tommy. The drug companies control everything. The data drives their decisions and the research, and they have criteria as far as who they want to measure."

"What if I go somewhere else to get it? You talked it up as some kind of miracle drug. What if I go to Mexico or something?"

"It's a trial, and not widely available. In fact, we're one of the few institutions that have it. Again, I'm sorry. Let's stay the course. We'll have other options eventually."

Tommy looked around the room again, weighing his options. *So tired of all of this.* "I'm getting tired, Doc. I feel so bad sometimes, I don't know what I'm doing this for. The trials are better than chemo, but the side effects, being cold all the time, skin cracking open, rashes, sore muscles, sores in my mouth, it's hell. What kind of way of living is this?"

"Hard living, but it beats the alternative, right? Again, we're just waiting for the next breakthrough. Then maybe it gets easier."

"I appreciate your positivity, but this is wearing me down. What about people that don't want to stay on the chemo, sick all the time, or die a slow and agonizing death? Isn't there some other option, some way to die with dignity? Some shot or pill to take to end it on our own terms when we've had enough?"

The doctor looked at him with interest. "Not officially. It's a social and religious hot button. There's a doctor...Kevorkian...he was actually doing that. They called him Dr. Death. The right-wingers demonized the guy and charged him with murder. You might remember, it was all over the news."

"Yeah. Actually, I remember the way it was portrayed. I was with the rest of the cops in my attitude toward it back then—lock the guy up, he's nuts. Now I got a whole different perspective. That's what I'd like. Maybe I can just go it on my own. Get a cabin up in the woods somewhere, bring my shotgun…"

"Tommy, don't say those things in front of me. It starts a whole other protocol."

"Jesus," Tommy said. "I guess we're not as free as we like to think, after all."

The doctor only nodded in response.

Tommy began to worry about the doctor reporting him, and getting him locked away in some kind of psych ward. "Anyway, I'm not saying I'm ready for that yet. I'm just wondering about options for when things start to get real bad. Until then, I got things I need to do. I just need a little more time. Can you juice me up again with the B12 and steroids, so I have some energy? Then I'll get out of your hair."

"Sure, that much I can do," Mason responded.

He remained silent while the doctor finished working on him. A prescription pad on the nearby counter caught his eye.

After his appointment, he went to the cafeteria for his meeting with Molletier. He found the man sitting alone at a table. A plate of untouched food sat before him, and he held a cup of steaming coffee between both hands.

"How'd yours go?" Tommy asked.

"Big news. I'm dying," he answered.

"Yeah, yeah. We know that. Join the club. Anything else?"

"Remission is over. New stuff growing in the garden inside of me. Back to chemo soon."

"Jesus, I'm sorry. Not much better for me. I have to find some way to keep my energy up, just for a little while. How the hell do you do it?"

"Ancient Asian herbs."

"I'm going to need some of those, then. We have work to do." Tommy filled him in on everything that had happened with Carson and Bobby.

The sensei listened attentively. "What are we going to do, then?" he asked when Tommy had finished.

"I'll come up with a plan. I'm not comfortable talking here. We'll get together soon at my place," Tommy said.

29 BALLOONS

TOMMY RETURNED the following day and made his way through the hospital entrance. *So sick of this place.* He carried a bag with some pictures and items from Bobby's room so that Bobby would feel more at home when he finally broke through the coma. He hoped it would happen while he was there. That was why he was spending every moment he could alongside his son.

As was his habit, he stopped at the coffee shop and stood in line. By the time he had reached the front, the young employee had his order ready. "Poppyseed bagel, toasted, strawberry spread, and a large black coffee, Mr. Borata," she proudly announced.

"You got it, kid. Right on the ball. Kids like you have a bright future in this world. Go out and make it a better place," Tommy said.

The colorful items in the hospital gift shop window caught his eye, and he entered. "Can I help you?" the woman behind the register asked. Her tone seemed hostile, as if he had come into her home unannounced. He looked at her, and she put down the book she had been reading. Her face was overly made up, in defiance of the years that had overtaken her, and her expression was dour.

"I'm just looking around if that's okay," Tommy replied.

He browsed, aware of her eyes on him, and after a time he became annoyed. He selected a bouquet of bright Mylar balloons and approached her. "What's the problem? You got a bug up your ass, lady?"

She twisted her face into a mask of shock. "Why, how dare you! I'll call security…" she stammered.

He pulled his wallet, making sure to expose the shield from his former occupation. "I *am* security, bitch. The real deal, not these rent-a-cops you got. Now ring me up so I can get outta here."

She hustled to complete his purchase, and he turned to stare her down before leaving.

He entered an elevator along with a few family members on their way to visit other patients. They carried happy, colorful gifts like his, but they all wore expressions of sadness. They all rode together, the elevator dispensing them at the various floors along the way. Each left without a word, lost in their own thoughts.

Getting off at Bobby's floor, he walked past the nurses' station. He knew them all by name now, but this time they were consumed in their work, and for the first time they didn't greet him cheerfully. "Why so quiet? Everybody having a bad day or something?" he asked as he made his way past.

Only one of them turned away from their tasks to acknowledge the comment with a nod. He sensed pity, and his stomach began to turn. He continued, rounded the final corner toward Bobby's room, and noticed a group in the hallway. *Margie. Diane. Carmen. All crying. Are the cops waiting for me in there? Maybe they know what I did to the guy's car?*

He quickened his pace, and they noticed him coming. Margie looked at him and turned away. Carmen started in his direction and intercepted him halfway there.

"Tommy, I'm so sorry," she said, hugging him.

And suddenly he realized. Logic would no longer allow alternative scenarios. "He's gone?" Tommy asked.

"I'm sorry," Carmen continued. "I was there, they tried everything. They tried so hard. I think he fought and fought. There was too much brain swelling, too much damage. I'm so sorry, Tommy."

"He's gone?" Tommy asked again, incredulous, unbelieving.

He pulled away, pushed her away from him. "He's really gone, Carmen?"

"Yes, Tommy. Yes. Please go to your wife, she needs you."

"That's something new. The thing is, I don't need anyone. Not her, not you. I got things to do that are more important than standing around here bawling with you people."

He let go of the balloons, letting them drift to the ceiling, and dropped the bag of items he was carrying. The elevator returned to the floor simultaneously, seeming to invite him, to take him to a different place. He entered it without looking back and stabbed a button with his finger.

In that moment, he felt everything leave him: the quest to be good; any love he had left for anyone or anything; the will to live. It was all replaced by a single need—to die someplace nice and then go to join his son and Moses in the hereafter, if there was one.

As he left the hospital and began his journey, he developed the first stages of his newly altered plan. He allowed himself a short time of mourning and decided he would move on after that, to accomplish his mission.

He thought of the highlights of the times he and Bobby had spent together. He replayed the boy's birth and his pride at having a son. He flipped through a selection of memories over the years, but the one he lingered on the longest, well longer than the time he had allotted, was a single recent night in a seedy bar.

His son's supportive acceptance of his bad news; his son's words of encouragement; his son's dreams of becoming an artist by the beach; his son's excitement at being accepted by him and finally moving on with his life in the open; his son standing under a single red spotlight, enthralling an entire room full of people, singing a classic blues song.

You damn sure made me proud, son. I'll never be the man you were, and that's all I ever hoped for, for you to exceed me. I'll see you soon, my sweet boy. We'll be together forever, someplace far better than this world.

30 THE FIGHT

SENSEI MOLLETIER WAITED silently from just inside the dark patch of trees bordering the strip-mall parking lot. The trees hid a grassy drainage catchment, which was in the center of the clearing behind him. He was dressed in his black Korean martial-arts uniform. It was well-worn and comfortable.

He took pride in being *godanja*, of high rank, and specifically *Ship-dan*, a rare tenth-degree black belt. He reflected on the lifetime of hard, disciplined training he had endured in his homeland to achieve his rank. *Long ago.*

He reached down and held the ends of the belt in his hands, fingering the fine Korean lettering inscribed into it. As he watched a large man lifting weights through the storefront window of the fitness center, he continued to journey through his past, wandering through the struggle of his family, oppressed by the North Korean regime. The sacrifices that his good parents had made, and the risks they took to escape to the South when he was a boy, all came to mind. Those were the happy years, with the family he loved, in the homeland that he loved.

Then he allowed himself to relive the tragedy of their death, and his long emigration process to America, and the struggle to establish himself, all while grieving every day. He had promised to never forget them, and to fight for oppressed people against tyranny, for his entire life. Until lately, he'd always felt that he hadn't lived up to that vow, other than to inject discipline and ethics into every student who came into his dojo, in hopes that they would go out into the world and make it a better place.

Now that his own end and the manner of his death were in sight, he felt truly virtuous for the first time and able to act on the years of pent-up hatred for those who bullied and hurt others.

He thought of the insecure, clumsy, overweight boy who had come into the studio with his overbearing father. He took the boy as far as he could and believed he had helped him, until he suddenly seemed to lose interest and stopped coming for instruction. *Young* jeja *Bobby, a good boy.* He thought about that boy, now dead because of the actions of a bully—the same man he watched through the fitness center window.

He felt the strain of anger building in his thoughts, and he suppressed it to focus on his target, his plan, and his intent. He questioned whether he should have included Borata in this, or told him, but he didn't want the distraction. He liked to work alone and not have to trust others, who were never as focused or disciplined as he was. *They make mistakes.*

This was his mission, and he was determined to bring justice to the man who had just finished his workout and gone through the door to the men's locker room. *They're closing soon. It won't be long.*

He gauged the distance to Carson's Porsche and went over the plan in his head again and again to pass the time. He wished that he had the strength and quickness of his earlier years, and hoped that his weakened body would hold out. *Back then, I would have destroyed him quickly.* He reminded himself to account for his lack of depth perception in choosing his tactics. He was prepared to spend himself on this, give everything he had, if necessary. His aim was not to kill, but to punish.

He began to try to stretch out his stiff muscles, saddened by how much weaker he was now, how much more tired than just a few months ago. He had always felt invincible, and now he couldn't deny that he was far from it. He went about his *kata* in slow motion: blocks, punches, kicks. Just enough to prepare his muscles, trying carefully to preserve whatever energy he had remaining.

~*~

Carson smiled at the fitness center receptionist on his way toward the exit. He stopped and leaned on her desk with an elbow, making sure to press his bicep against his ribs to accentuate its size. "Given any thought to going away with me for a few days?" he asked her. "Wherever you want to go; you name it."

She continued looking at her computer screen. "I'm still happily married, so that's a no," she said in a dismissive tone.

"C'mon. That's what business trips are for, right? Tell him you're going to research another location for the gym."

"I'm busy, Carson. Give it a break, okay?"

His flirtatious demeanor switched to anger in a split second. "Fine. Your loss, honey. Drive safe and obey the speed limit, know what I'm saying?"

She ignored him, and he ignored the laughter behind him, leaving in a huff and upset that his good mood had been lost. He made his way across the parking lot to his car, parked at the perimeter to avoid dents from others.

His limbs ached from the aggressive workout, and he was exhausted from the preceding twelve-hour shift. *I'll take a swing by that gay club on the way home, wait in the parking lot to see if that Mike dude is around.*

He pressed the unlock button on his key fob and thought he heard another sound beneath its squawk and the clunk of the door unlocking. He turned in a circle, scanning his surroundings. Then he heard it again.

"Carson."

The voice came from just inside the woods. He moved a little closer and debated retrieving his service weapon from the glove box. Curiosity got the better of him, and he took a few more steps.

"Come on. Come closer. Be brave," the eerie voice implored.

He cautiously moved closer. As his eyes adjusted, he spotted a bald Asian man in a karate uniform a short distance away, standing under moonlight in a clearing just past the trees. The man was missing an eye, the blank socket covered with stretched scar tissue.

"Oh, shit. If it ain't Bruce Lee," he said.

"Let's go. Man on man," the man continued. "I'm unarmed." He held his arms out.

"Molletier, right? The guy with Borata, teaching karate to those spooks in the park? What's your beef, buddy?" Carson asked. He thought again about going to the car for his firearm. *Maybe not. I'm in enough trouble, anyway. I can't shoot him, but I can kick his ass. This is too good to pass up. Priceless.*

"You like to hurt people, Carson. Let's see how you like to get hurt."

Carson processed several theories. "Who sent you—Borata? Is this about his kid? Tell that old man to fight his own battles."

"I'll tell him you were afraid of me. You like to pick on old men and people weaker than yourself. You're a coward, in your heart. I can always smell it."

Carson's anger returned. *I don't get enough chances to kick ass these days.* "Your kung-fu bullshit won't help you, dumbass. You know about the new stuff? Cage fighting? You're about to find out." He dropped his workout bag and headed toward the man, who immediately took a fighting stance.

Carson laughed, now excited, and charged. He decided to go low for a quick takedown and get it over with, so he could be on his way. As he started to lower himself and reach for Molletier's legs, he yelled, "I'll fuck you up—"

He didn't get to finish the sentence. He saw a flash of movement, heard a swish of air and clothing, and his head exploded into a swirling cluster of tiny points of light.

He staggered sideways, losing his balance, and backed up to reassess. His opponent stood back. "Alright, douchebag. Maybe I underestimated you. Let's go again." This time he approached more cautiously, guard up, looking for a way to grab and grapple the smaller man in order to make the most of his size advantage.

Molletier kept his calm demeanor and stared at Carson intently from behind his fighting stance. "Come at me, bitch. Come on," Carson taunted. The man didn't move. Carson went at him again, a little slower this time, and was bringing his big leg up for a side-kick when the man seemed to levitate into a short jump, twisting sideways, and plant a foot deep into his solar plexus, taking his wind away.

He backed up again, gasping for air, and felt blood running from his eyebrow into his right eye, taking away half his vision with it. He wiped at it, and charged again, raging. He grabbed at the man and had a handful of his clothing when he felt himself sailing upside down over the man's body. He landed on his back, vulnerable, yet the man didn't come at him to take advantage.

That's a mistake. He jumped up, his stomach aching from the kick.

Taking stock, he now noticed that the man was attempting to hide his heavy breathing. *That's why he didn't keep coming. He's out of gas. Out of shape. Trying to conserve energy. Bingo.* Carson calmed himself, strategizing. "I'm too big for you, little man. Too young. Too fit. You're fast but old and sick, like your buddy. You're out of shape," he taunted, circling. He moved in, waited for Molletier to counter, then backed up. He kept him moving as much as he could.

He feinted low, then rose up and blocked the kick he knew would come. While Molletier was slightly off-balance, he was able to grab a handful of his shirt. He pulled the man into him, taking space away, and reached to get a hold with his other hand.

Molletier executed a crisp block, ripping his grip away, sent a short kick to his knee, buckling it, then backed away to regain his buffer.

Carson hobbled a few steps, still circling. *He's trying to disable me limb by limb, using as little energy as he can. I'm too big; he's not hurting me as much as he figured.* He psyched himself, bouncing on the balls of his feet. He came in, leading with a straight kick. Molletier blocked it, and Carson took advantage of his taller stature by landing a downward punch to the man's head. His fist stung, but he saw the man stagger slightly and step back, reaching the edge of the drainage pit, then lose his balance and tumble backward down the slope.

Carson leaped forward, hopping down the hill to try to catch his adversary as he rolled down the incline. Molletier tumbled himself intentionally, trying to pick up speed so he could get to the bottom and regroup. Carson tried to chase, limping down the hill as fast as he could without falling.

Molletier reached bottom and was beginning to spring up when Carson took a risk and dove at him, making contact and driving them both down into the shallow water at the bottom of the drainage pit. The man struggled to free himself, but now Carson had the advantage in strength and size. He was atop his opponent, who was face-down. Carson moved quickly, leveraging his grappling expertise to tie up the man's limbs. He slipped his arm under the other man's, then brought his hand back over Molletier's neck, driving his head into the water.

"You want to die here, motherfucker? You want to die tonight?" His adrenaline was surging, and he was angry at being harmed, at ruining his favorite, expensive workout clothing, at being challenged. He wanted to kill. He pulled Molletier's head back up. "You hear me, gook? Answer!"

"Go ahead. Kill me. I'm dead already," Molletier answered.

"Pussy. I thought you were a tough guy. Not so tough now, are you?" Carson drove the man's head down into the water again and held it there, enjoying his domination but wanting to enjoy someone begging for their life, his favorite part. Molletier stopped struggling, and Carson realized he had lost track of how long he'd held him under.

He pulled the man's head back up and found it limp. Fear swept through him as he worried he'd killed him. He grabbed Molletier's belt and dragged him back up the hill, flipping him over. As soon as he'd rolled the man onto his back, a foot shot up and caught him on the nose and mouth, snapping his head back.

Carson flew into a rage again and dropped down, punching the defenseless man in the head. When he saw the bloody mess on the man's face, he stopped. This time he made sure Molletier was truly unconscious but breathing.

He dragged him up further up the slope to level ground and sat him up against the base of a tree. He took the karate belt off and tied it around Molletier's neck and the tree, making sure it was just tight enough to allow a limited amount of air as long as he didn't struggle when he came to, and out of reach to untie the knot.

He got into his truck and drove. As he expected, when he reached his destination he found the Black Eagles loitering outside.

Lukas rose up and motioned for the others to stay put as he walked over. Carson rolled his window down.

"Tell your friend Borata he can find his chink buddy tied to a tree over by the gym on Maple

Street. He better hurry. And tell him I'll be talking to him very soon."

He raised the window and peeled off down the street.

IKE SAT NERVOUSLY on Tommy's couch. "I've never been to this part of town. It's kind of unnerving."

Tommy reached for his cup of coffee. "You know what?" he replied, "There's better people here than anywhere else in this city. Definitely better people than the ones in the rich neighborhoods. These people work hard and don't have much to show for it. They enjoy the simple things. They love each other like I remember people used to do. You're safe here."

"Okay, but I can't stay long."

"We don't need much time. Hopefully, the sensei got my messages and will be here soon. I haven't been able to reach him for days. We all have to avoid contact. The first thing I have to ask is, are you sure about this? Absolutely sure?"

"I am. All my life, people like us have been made miserable by people like him. All the way back as far as I can remember. I'm going to do this for me, and for Bobby. That cop's got to pay."

"Listen, then. All you know is that you met the cop at the club that night, he gave you his info, and you agreed to meet him. Nothing more, nothing less, you got it? You weren't aware that anything else was going to happen. You can even say that you mentioned it to me. That puts the focus on me. I'll be gone, so I don't care."

Mike gave Tommy a determined look. "Got it."

"I'm not telling you about anything or anybody else related to this. Just get Carson there, and keep him talking. You don't know anything else."

"Okay."

"Alright. So what's next for you, Mike?"

"I don't have any family around here. They're all Midwestern religious zealots. All I had around here was my job and Bobby. There's nothing more for me here, now that he's gone. I sold off my half of the garage to my business partner." He began to cry, and Tommy put an arm around him, fighting back his own emotion.

"I'll make this right. Carson will pay. Don't say where you're going. Not to me or anyone."

"I got it," Mike said, collecting himself.

"Good luck, Mike. This is the last time we'll talk."

They stood and embraced. After Mike was gone, Tommy sat in silence, energizing himself by going through the plan in his mind. He thought about Moses, his son, his new life, his disease. He felt at peace, despite the underlying, agonizing grief. He worked to hold it in check until his work was done.

A short time later, another knock sounded at the door. It alarmed him since he hadn't heard the footsteps on the stairs that announced his visitors. He got up silently and peered through the peephole in the door. When he opened it, he stared in shock at Molletier.

"Sensei, what the hell happened to you? Were you out driving around again?" he tried to joke. He opened the door wider and helped the man in.

"How the hell did you get here? I didn't hear a car outside."

"It's not important. I appear when I need to appear. I'm healing, but still pretty sore." Molletier gave him scant details about what had happened, how Lukas had gone to rescue him, how he made him vow to not involve Tommy or disturb his grief that night.

Tommy shook his head angrily throughout the story, looking Molletier over. His face was completely black and blue, with splotches of yellow, green, and purple in some areas. His nose was clearly broken, a deep, scabbed-over gash at the bridge of it. His lips were split in several places, and he still had welts on his forehead and cheekbones. His black eye patch was the only unscathed part of his face. "Jesus, shouldn't you be in the hospital?"

"Sick of the hospital. I have Asian medicine. Better than your American hospitals."

"You sure nothing's broke?"

"Nose, some teeth. Can't do much about those. This will heal, the cancer will not. I'm almost done with this body, with this life. I have only one purpose now."

Tommy felt an overwhelming sense of sadness. He felt like he was back where he'd been with Moses, just before they were supposed to execute their plan to take out the priest. Many times he'd regretted not calling everything off at that stage, thinking Moses would still be alive, before he remembered the man's advancing disease. *It's how he wanted to go.*

"Look, Sensei. Why don't we just call this off? Carson will eventually get his. We have enough on our plates."

The anger on the man's broken, distorted face made his answer clear even before he spoke. "No. This must be done. You can stand down. I will avenge myself and Bobby alone if I must."

"Okay, okay. That was a test, I'm sorry. I had to make sure. One more thing. Three times now you've ignored our plans and gone off alone. We can't have that this time. It's just a few of us, and if we don't all do exactly what we say, it will fall apart, and we're all screwed."

"I understand the plan."

"No, no. None of that 'I understand the plan' routine. I've heard that before, too many times. Sensei, I need your word of honor, as a man, on your reputation, that you will do this exactly as we planned it out together. There's a lot more at stake this time. It has to go right."

"You have my word. My word is as good as my life. How much time do you figure until they find him?"

"He's on leave, and he's kind of a loner, so hopefully not until sometime late the next day. Alright, then. This is the last time we'll talk. What's next for you? I did some work with the witness protection program. I know how to make people disappear if that's what they want. You interested in the Florida Keys?"

Molletier shook his head. "I will go to Korea immediately. Back to my home. Everything is arranged. It is there that I wish to die. I want to see my homeland one more time."

"Alright, then. Tomorrow night is it. We won't get a chance to say goodbye. I wish you luck, Sensei. Thank you for everything you've done for Bobby, and for me."

They both stood, slowly and painfully, and Tommy showed him out.

Shortly after, he heard footsteps on the stairs. He rose and unlocked the deadbolts once more to let Lukas in. Whitey followed behind him and jumped immediately onto Tommy's lap.

"How's the franken-bike coming along?"

"Good as gold. Well, maybe copper. Maybe rusted iron. It's ugly, but it's done. I've been scrounging parts from everywhere within two hundred miles. Using the disguises, of course."

"You're good to go then?" Tommy asked, petting the affectionate dog.

"I'm all set. You sure he won't bring anyone or set you up?"

"Nah. The last thing that asshole wants is for anyone to know he's a closet gay. His ego is too big, and that's gonna be his downfall. What's your plan for after this?"

"I'm staying here. This is my home. If it gets too hot, I'll bug out, I have places I can go. Tass and I want to get married."

"You didn't…" Tommy began.

"None of the Eagles know. None of them. Not even her."

"Okay, then. You know that your uncle is looking down on you. Remember, all you know is that you built me a bike. I wanted to ride again."

"Well, that's all you really told me anyway, Tommy. What about you? You leaving after this?" Lukas asked.

"I'll get away if I can. Somewhere nice, to die alone. If they do arrest me, I'll lawyer up and drag it out for a long time. The doc figures I have less than a year anyway, and that's being optimistic.

"I'm telling you, and I told the others, I'll take the fall for this. What're they gonna do, give me the death sentence? I'll probably go into hiding—someplace nice. I have options. I have a lot of contacts from when I was on the job, all over the country."

They embraced for a long time. Lukas pulled away and went through the door, leaving Tommy to his thoughts and plans.

32 THE SETUP

OMMY SAT ON THE MOTORCYCLE, peering through the night with binoculars. The bike's engine purred almost inaudible at low idle. Its muffler was packed to quiet it, and its lights were disconnected. He swiveled to check the darkest, furthest corner of the parking lot, where Mike's jacked-up pickup truck was parked. Mike sat behind the wheel, and even from that distance, Tommy could sense his nervousness. *Stay cool, buddy. Don't blow it.*

He tilted the binoculars lower. There was only darkness under the pickup. He knew that Molletier was lying prone under it, watching and waiting for the signal. *He's got to be hurting, lying under there in his condition.* He scanned the rest of the parking lot and club. *Pretty empty, good. No witnesses.* He checked his watch. *Almost midnight.*

He mentally calculated the distance from the back of the pickup, across the empty lot adjacent to the club's parking lot, to the empty warehouse on the other side. *Just like the warehouse you hurt my son in, Carson. All we need now is you, the star of the show.*

He beat back the waves of nausea, pain, and cold that wracked his body, determined to execute the plan with precision. Finally, he saw Carson's Porsche approach from a distance, its lights off. It came to a stop, and he knew Carson was assessing the situation. Mike gave a small wave to him from the cab of the pickup. Tommy ducked down further, hoping his bike wasn't visible. They had tested all of this out, but somehow the light from the parking lot seemed brighter, and there was less cloud cover to obscure the moon. *Can't help anything now. It's show time.*

Carson's vehicle crept forward, slowly approaching and then stopping until it was fully in the parking lot, exposed. He knew Carson had to be making his final decision at this point. *His dick and his ego will win over his brain.*

The Porsche drove over to Mike's pickup and parked, leaving an empty space between them. Tommy watched as Carson exited and walked over to Mike's open driver-side window and they began a conversation.

Movement in the direction Carson's car had come from caught his eye. He saw a police car approaching from the road. *Jesus, no.* He turned back to Carson and Mike and saw that Carson was now crouched next to Mike's truck. Mike must have laid down in the front seat, out of sight. Tommy's heart was racing, as he knew everyone else's must have been.

I can't afford a fucking heart attack right now. He turned back to the cruiser and watched as it entered the parking lot. He ran the scenarios through his mind, wondering if Carson had set up a search of the club or whether he was onto their plan and set up a takedown of them. Neither would be a desirable outcome.

He briefly considered how he might pull the plug on the plan and get everyone away safely, but there was no option. In their confidence, they hadn't formulated a bail-out scenario. If they were going down, they were all going down together. *I got to pull this off, for Bobby.*

The cruiser was now circling the building, a relief to Tommy. *Just a routine patrol, checking things out. One lap and he'll move on.*

But as the cruiser came around the building, instead of leaving it stopped, facing them all but fortunately not from a position where it could see Carson. Tommy could see the glow of a phone lighting up inside the police car. The officer was making a call. For several long, agonizing minutes he watched as the officer carried on a casual conversation with someone, laughing periodically.

He heard voices and peeked up to see two men exiting the bar. *What now.* They walked to a car facing Mike's truck, where Carson was clearly in view of them. If they hadn't been so absorbed in each other, they would've surely seen Carson crouching next to it. Tommy watched and listened as they flirted, each wanting the same thing, both tentative. *For chrissake, somebody make a move.* They began making out, and then he heard the door locks pop. Both men got into the car.

When the driver started it and turned on his headlights, Carson was briefly illuminated until the driver turned to leave the lot. Adrenaline surged as Tommy checked to make sure Carson was watching the departing car, and not looking in his direction.

He checked back to where the police car had been, and the cop was now gone. Carson stood back up, and he and Mike were back in conversation. *Keep him occupied, Mike. Just a few more minutes.*

Tommy took one more visual sweep of the area, and everything looked good. He picked up the binoculars again and focused in on Carson's feet. *All set; now or never.* He withdrew a laser pointer from his jacket pocket and pointed it beneath the truck. He pressed the button to give two flashes of light, then picked the binoculars back up from his neck strap.

Tommy noticed a shift of movement and looked above the binoculars. Carson seemed to catch the laser's beam from the corner of his eye and was looking his way. *Oh, shit.* He looked back through the binoculars at Carson's feet, just long enough to see Molletier's hands extend from below the truck and snap a cuff onto one of his ankles. Mike immediately started the truck and backed up, exposing a long length of stainless steel cable attached to the cuff on Carson's ankle and leading to the darkness of the abandoned lot next to the parking area. Molletier, now exposed, began to rise from his prone position, smiling at Carson.

Carson looked at him, then down in surprise at his leg, and tried to run. The cable stretched taut between his foot and the other end at the back frame of Tommy's bike. Tommy felt a tug as Carson tumbled to the pavement. *Fish on the line.*

Tommy turned back to the bike, revved the throttle, and popped the clutch. The bike lurched and then stalled. In a panic, he pushed the starter button, looking back toward Carson. He'd regained his feet and was yanking at Mike's door, trying to open it, but Mike had thankfully raised the window and locked it.

Tommy continued to try to start the bike, and then heard the death groan of the starter motor as the battery died. He looked back—Carson was now straining to reach for his own car door. *That's where his phone and gun are.* Tommy felt the bike being tugged backward by Carson's sheer strength and jammed it into gear to try to stop it. *Damn it. We're fucked.*

Something suddenly clicked in his addled, diseased mind. Something from long ago, back in his own riding days as a happy teenager mounting his own barely running Triumph to go into town in search of girls to impress. His leg followed the muscle memory and slid down the side frame of the bike, and he found the kickstart lever exactly where it should be. He flipped it out with his foot, and with all of the strength he could summon, he rose up and then threw his entire weight down onto the lever, simultaneously pulling in the clutch and twisting the throttle at just the right moment.

The bike burst to life with a muted roar, and he looked back once more to see Carson turning in his direction to see what the noise was, his hand having just reached the door to his Porsche. Tommy popped the clutch again and twisted the throttle, this time pulling the bike up into a wheelie and on its way across the vacant lot.

The front wheel came back down, and the large man behind him was suddenly yanked into the air, then slammed down to the parking lot. His body was dragged behind Tommy's bike across the trash-strewn lot toward the warehouse, twisting and rolling. *Adios, motherfucker. This one's for Bobby. Enjoy the ride, roadkill.*

33 REVENGE

TOMMY PULLED the sputtering bike into the warehouse and quickly hopped off. Despite the cold sweat dripping from his head through to his feet, he was careful not to remove his helmet, heavy jacket, or gloves.

He walked the length of the steel cable attached to the rear of the motorcycle until the other end appeared. He peered through the dark to assess how much of Carson was left, and whether he was still alive.

The big man's clothes were mostly stripped from his body, and a great deal of his skin was gone from the half-mile drag through the vacant lots behind the bike. He reminded Tommy of a large side of beef in the meat warehouse, dark red and raw.

Tommy bent down toward the man's head to listen for any sound or breath. At that moment, a rattle and gurgle emerged from the unrecognizable face, and an arm twitched. "So, you're still alive, motherfucker. Good. You hear me, bitch?"

He kicked the man in the ribs, eliciting a groan and more gurgling and rattling. "You trying to say something, Carson? Big tough man, aren't you? Can't talk? Talk to me, asshole. You always had a lot to say before. Did you like your rough ride? I think I give a better rough ride than you, don't I?"

Tommy began to worry about time. They'd planned for no wasted time, in case someone called the police about the suspicious activity in the parking lot. He stared down at Carson, who was beginning to make horrendous, inhuman sounds. "Goodbye, human scum. This is from me, and Bobby, and every poor bastard whose life you made miserable. Time to go, Carson. Meet your maker, you miserable son of a bitch."

He placed his boot on the man's throat, and stood on it, applying as much weight as he could without losing his balance. When the choking sounds stopped, and he leaned into it further, he heard the soft cracking sounds of vertebrae, like distant twigs being stepped on in a forest.

He bent down and listened again until he was satisfied, then issued another kick to the man's ribs. It was like kicking an overstuffed bag of garbage. No response.

He produced a key, removed the leg cuff and wound the cable back up, tying it to the motorcycle's luggage rack. He mounted the bike and drove off.

When he was a block away from the salvage yard, he cut the engine and rolled the bike in. The gate was unlocked, as Lukas had promised it would be. He put the bike under the large sheets of scrap metal that Lukas had shown him, next to the massive car-crushing machine that would dispose of it the next day. He removed all of his clothing, boots, and gear and placed them into the burn barrel, and changed into what had been left for him in the plastic bag under the metal. He picked up the nearby gas can, doused the barrel, and then lit and threw in a match.

His part done, he walked toward the salvage yard exit. The moon was out and seemed to smile down on him. *What a nice night.*

34 EXIT

THANKS FOR SQUEEZING ME IN before office hours, Doc," Tommy said. His mind was spinning, and he struggled to not allow his exhaustion and grief to overtake him. He didn't want to tip off the doctor.

Dr. Carson sat back in his chair. "No problem, but we can only take a few minutes. So, you're refusing to go with the chemo?"

"That's right," Tommy said adamantly. "No more of that. The cure is worse than the disease."

"The disease is terminal, Tommy."

"I get that. I don't want to go out that way. It's not for me. It'll disable me, and I have things I still need to do. I might have to travel; I have an undercover work opportunity I'm interested in."

The comment caused the doctor to raise an eyebrow.

"What are my other options?" Tommy asked. "What would *you* do if you were in my shoes?"

"The best thing I can think of is to try to go back on the original medicine you were on. We had good results with that; your type of cancer reacted to it well. You've been off it long enough that the resistance you developed may be gone now."

"Can you give me enough to get me through a few months?"

"Tommy, you can't go that long without checking in so that we can monitor your progress. It's a requirement for the drug."

"Okay, I can do that," he lied. "Can you give me a script for a month then, and we'll see how it goes?" The doctor appeared reluctant, and Tommy added: "I can check in by phone in two weeks."

"I suppose, Tommy." The doctor wrote the script, along with one for nausea and one for self-administered steroid injections, and handed them to him.

Tommy thanked him and left the room as quickly as civility would allow. He went directly to his car and got to work, using the skills that decades on the force had taught him about forgery to fill out the two clean pages he had stolen from Dr. Mason's prescription pad. His disease and treatment, the stuffiness in the car, and above all the grief that he was trying to suppress were building his nausea to a crescendo, and he fought it off. When he had finished, he turned to the passenger seat and asked Molletier if he was ready.

They re-entered the hospital and waited outside the pharmacy until it started to get busy, then went in and got into line. When he had worked his way to the front, he handed the prescription over.

The pharmacist examined it. "Forbaxatel. I don't normally see a prescription for this amount of this drug," he said under his breath.

"Yeah, I just came from the doc. I've got to go somewhere warmer for a while, and I'll be seeing another doc while I'm away. He wanted to make sure I didn't run out, or have availability problems there. It's kind of a rural place."

"I understand. I'm just going to call upstairs to verify."

Tommy tried to think quickly, and he was getting sicker by the moment. "Hey, listen, I'm in a bit of a hurry, not feeling well at all. I have to get that stuff into me, and the other one for the nausea meds. Stat."

"Just a moment," the man said, picking up the phone.

He looked back at Molletier, thinking of the ridiculous risk they had taken. He was about to signal a quick departure when he noticed the pharmacist looking frustrated while waiting for someone to answer.

"Nobody's answering," he said to Tommy. "It's early and they may not be in yet, or making the rounds. Would you mind waiting?"

"Listen," Tommy answered. "I got to get home, get my fellow patient here home, and get these meds in me. Besides, I'm having the shits about every half hour from all of this, and nauseous as hell. You don't want a mess to clean up. My buddy here is going on the trip with me, he's got the same script. He's in the same trial."

Molletier moved forward and gave the man his prescription. "We got to leave, very sick. Check with doctor later, please."

The line behind them was growing, and people were beginning to grumble. Finally, the pharmacist went to the dispensary and came back with the filled drugs.

They hurried across the parking lot, white paper bags in hand. "You want me to drive?" Molletier asked.

"Good God, no," Tommy answered. They got into his car and drove as quickly as the speed limit would allow, first to drop Molletier off at the airport with his bags, and then to his apartment. He checked carefully for any hidden police presence before entering the block. He parked a distance away, approached on foot through back alleys, and then climbed up the fire escape ladder that he had left in the lowered position.

Inside his apartment, he quickly packed an old sea bag from his Marine days, with a few essentials and all of the cash that he had been withdrawing from his accounts over the past few days. The last items he placed inside it were the two white paper bags from the pharmacy. *Thanks once more, Molletier. This should be enough to see me through for a while, anyway.*

When the sea bag was ready, he sat down at the same kitchen table that his friend Moses had written his suicide note at, and using the same pad and pen wrote several letters himself: one to his wife apologizing for the bad years; one to Carmen thanking her for her care; and one a suicide note to all concerned.

He moved to the living room and sat on the same ragged couch that had belonged to Moses. As he surveyed the room, his mind flooded with memories of their times together there—good and bad. He pictured his friend sitting in his usual chair, smoking a joint and enjoying his music. *See you soon, friend. It's all I have to look forward to now. Just a little more business to attend to first.*

He rose and gathered his things, then climbed out and hustled down the fire escape with the sea bag as quickly as his tortured body would allow. The Eagles were still at work, and he wanted to get out without encountering anyone.

When he reached the alley, he walked down it with the sea bag slung over his shoulder, in the direction of the setting sun. Whitey poked his head from the top of the bag and licked the back of Tommy's neck.

3 ARRIVAL

TOMMY DOMINGO UNPACKED the contents of his seabag while his faithful dog lay watching in the doorway. A gentle breeze flowed through the small cottage's windows and felt soothing on his skin. He could hear the sound of the ocean nearby and smelled the salt in the air. *Very therapeutic. Not a bad place to die.*

He stopped and sat on the simple metal frame bed to catch his breath. His dog leaped up and settled in next to him. When he had recovered, he spread all of his belongings out, making sure that there was no trace of his previous identity. He placed his semi-automatic weapon and two boxes of ammunition in one of the weathered dresser's drawers.

He examined the few pieces of fake ID that he'd bought back in the city from the one underworld person that he trusted, paying a sufficient price to guarantee silence. The picture on the laminated card, a very aged and weathered-looking old man, stared back at him. The name on it was still new to him. *Thomas Domingo.* He burned it into his brain, forcing himself to dismiss who he used to be and accept this new person. *Just for whatever time I have left.*

He unscrewed the top of a prescription bottle and shook out one of the large pills inside. *Don't tell me I can't have some damn Forbaxatel.* He opened another with Korean writing on it and extracted a seaweed-green pill. He washed them down with a splash of tap water from the faucet, the rank aftertaste of the green pill lingering in his mouth. *Damn it, Sensei. This stuff better work, at least for a little while.* Looking out of the windows, he saw only jungle-type brush and trees in every direction. *No neighbors.*

He was thankful that the landlord was in a different state, had agreed to set everything up over the phone and keep all utilities in his name in exchange for a sizable wired deposit and six months of rent in advance.

The sea bag was almost empty. He extracted a folder and took out a photograph of a younger version of himself, standing with his arm around a large young man in a police uniform. He propped it up on the stand next to his bed, where he could see it in the dim light. A folded-up, tattered poster of Bob Marley followed that, and he carefully installed it on the wall with a few of the old thumb tacks that were stuck in the wood. Next, he pulled out a bottle in a brown paper sack. He unscrewed the top and took a long drink from it. He sat the bottle next to the bed and wiped his mouth with his sleeve. *Mad dog. That's me.*

Lying down on the thin mattress, he closed his eyes, and the memories began to wash over him. He could no more suppress them than he could suppress the cold chills, pain, and nausea from his disease and the medicines he took for it.

It was quiet, except for the rustling of the palm trees in the breeze, and it took him away to his dreams.

The End

Preview: Book III: The Candidate

THOMAS BRAND WATCHED from his office window above as a woman waited to cross a busy intersection in the relentless downpour. She juggled her umbrella and a grocery bag while holding her child's hand. A driver slowed, motioning her across, and she jumped at the opportunity, hurrying with her son into the street.

Another driver approached from the opposite direction and braked hard at the last second, blaring his horn at them. It startled the woman; she paused briefly in panic and then pulled her son into a quick trot.

She reached the curb, stumbling as she looked back to ensure her son could negotiate it safely. She released his hand so he wouldn't be pulled down with her as she fell hard to the sidewalk. Her bag of groceries spilled onto the wet concrete as her umbrella was blown inside-out and flew out of her grasp. She attempted to regain her feet as her child cried beside her.

Brand erupted in laughter. "Oh, Jesus. I wish I had a video of this shit. Brenda, Harry, come over and check out this elephant wallowing around on the sidewalk. She looks like a hippo at the watering hole on National Geographic. It's priceless."

"Sir, please," Brenda replied. "We've got to focus. The interview is in a few hours. The whole country will be watching, and this network airtime is critical. Please come and sit down so that we can rehearse your talking points."

Harry Stinson rose obediently and stood next to Brand at the window. "I hope she's not hurt," he said.

"Come on, Stinson. She's well padded—a fat fuck like you," Brand said, jabbing the man's arm. "That's some funny shit though, watching fat people fall and try to get up. It's like in the old comedies, before everyone got politically correct, right?"

Stinson didn't answer, and Brand continued. "Check out her kid. Fucking half-and-half. See, this is what I mean. That's why we need to win the nomination and the presidency. We're losing our damn country. We're losing our white identity. The Democrats encourage all this race-mixing, letting the queers run around in the open, and they want to let every filthy immigrant into the country. Anything goes with these liberals."

Brand peered through the rain-splashed glass. "All my hard work to keep my late father's empire smoothly running is what made me a wealthy man. I have to turn over too much of my hard-earned cash to the government just so rabble like that can get a check in the mail every month for doing nothing. I bet that bag of food she just wasted came from food stamps I paid for.

"Stinson, pour me another bourbon, please."

"Which is why this meeting is so important," Brenda insisted. "Please, let's sit down and do the mock interview. They're going to push you, try to get you to say something controversial so they can make you look bad. Like what you just *said*, for example. You shouldn't be so candid, even in places or among people you believe you can trust."

"I'm not worried about that, not here in my office with you two, anyway." Brand returned to the leather executive chair behind his large carved maple desk. Stinson placed a full tumbler on the blotter, took a seat next to Brenda, and picked his notepad and pen up from the floor.

"Good," Brenda said. "I'm going to play the interviewer. Harry, jot down anything we should review later, but don't interrupt our flow. We'll go over it point-by-point after we're done. I'll start the machine now." She pressed a button on the recorder.

"Welcome to our viewers. I'm Brenda Mallory with Signal News Network. We're here with Republican presidential candidate Thomas Brand, ahead of the widely anticipated Republican primary debate. Sir, welcome."

"Thank you, Brenda. I'm a big fan of your network, but I say that to all the networks, and I despise all of them. I can't wait to be president and shut down the media like they did in Russia. I'm also a big fan of your lovely ass and big tits." He laughed again, slapping his desk, and Stinson followed suit until a glare from Brenda shut them down.

"If we're not going to be serious, I'm out of here," she said angrily. "Or better yet, I'll insist that your wife sit in on these meetings."

"Alright, alright. Can't we have a little fun while we're doing all this boring shit?" Brand picked up a remote control and turned on a large television hanging from the opposite wall. "Let's see what they're saying about me today. That's more important than playing these stupid games."

~*~

Tommy Domingo scratched his thick white beard. He considered shaving it to relieve the constant itching but didn't want to risk being identified. He lay down on the bed in his sparse bungalow. An ocean breeze blew through the windows, pleasantly cooling the sweat on his skin. It was too hot and humid for Whitey to join him as he typically did, so the dog gazed at him from the cool tile floor in the bathroom.

He reflected on his decision to abruptly leave his doctors, chemo treatments, and cheating wife behind to spend the remainder of his time quietly alone in the Keys. *And I missed my son's funeral. My poor Bobby.*

"I guess we had no choice, Whitey. No sense in waiting around for them to figure out I killed that corrupt cop and show up to bust me. I do miss Nurse Carmen, though. It's just you and me now, and this ain't a bad place to die.

"This is the life Bobby wanted. He and I should be here together. He just wanted to ditch the rat race and be a guy on the sidewalk creating spray-paint art. Why the hell do people spend their lives sitting in traffic and shoveling snow, when they could live somewhere like here? Why did I, come to think of it?"

He rose, went into the kitchen, and filled Whitey's water dish with fresh, cool water from the tap, then scraped the remains of a can of dog food into his food bowl. He unscrewed the cap of a large orange prescription bottle and took one of the pills inside, washing it down with a handful of water. He inspected the label. *Forbaxatel. Take with food.* "We're both almost out of the grub we brought with us, buddy. I guess we better finally venture out of here to restock."

He went to the rust-speckled refrigerator and removed a large bottle of wine, holding it up to the window to inspect its level. "More importantly, we're almost out of vino." He tipped the bottle up and guzzled a large quantity. "Fruit of the vine, Whitey. A gift from God…or whoever."

Whitey ran from the bathroom to the kitchen for his treasure as Tommy moved to a rattan couch in the living room. He sat on its thin, flimsy cushions with his bottle and turned on the television. He leaned forward to adjust the antenna, bringing the picture into focus just as the evening news was beginning.

Tommy reached beneath the couch and pulled out a tin cigar box. Pulling the lid off with a metallic pop, he examined the layers of cellophane bags neatly rolled inside. He lifted it to his nose, closed his eyes and inhaled. "Oh damn, Whitey. Why did I ever waste so much time smoking cigs when this stuff was available? Thank you, Moses, for the stash. Rest in peace, my friend."

He tried to place it on the coffee table and misjudged, spilling the box onto the floor. As he picked up the tin to refill it, he noticed a folded paper in the bottom. He pulled it out and read it carefully.

Friend Tommy,

We talked a lot in the chemo ward about being able to die on our own terms, so I wanted to give you a parting gift. I put this in your stash box before you left so that you'd find it when you probably need it most—when your marijuana was almost gone. You only need one, but I left you two, just in case you screw it up and lose or break one. Take it straight for a more immediate effect or dilute it if you wish. I hope you never need to use it, but I know if the time comes, you'll want it, as I'm sure I will also.

Your friend,

Sensei Molletier

He searched the floor, picking up the rolled bags of pot and placing them back into the cigar box. When he had replaced them all, he slid off the couch slowly, grunting with the effort. On his knees, he searched again, this time spotting two small black vials beneath the coffee table. He retrieved them and sat back on the couch, turning them over in his hand. They had identical white labels with Korean lettering.

The news anchor had moved on to coverage of the presidential primaries. "The surprising rise of West Virginia businessman Thomas Brand and his ascent to the top three Republican candidates has gotten the country's attention. His far-right views have served as a divisive factor within the party and across the nation."

The scene cut to a Brand campaign rally, where a large crowd of fired-up supporters raised their fists and cheered at everything the candidate said from his pulpit on the stage. A large banner that read "Brand Brigade" was held above a group of men and women. The banner featured a Confederate flag on one side of the lettering, and "White Power" with a clenched fist on the other. Some in the group sported Nazi symbols. *How many of our people died fighting that garbage, and now this closet racist stands for it.*

The candidate was railing against the scourge of homosexuality that he claimed was poisoning society's values. Tommy thought of his gentle son and what he must have endured during his life because of homophobes like Brand and the corrupt cop Carson that had caused Bobby's death.

At that moment, he saw the root of all of the evil that had tortured and tormented less fortunate people like his son and late African-American friend Moses for their entire lives. People like Brand, who lavished themselves with riches, gorging on the fruits of their wealth with no sense of charity, viewing those less fortunate with disdain. *I'd like to cut the head off that evil snake.*

A black protester had been detected near the front of the audience by the candidate, who then urged the crowd to remove him. The camera shot zoomed in to show the man being hustled toward the exit by large security guards. He was shoved and spit on by the people under the banner as he passed them.

Tommy felt his anger grow and began talking to the screen. "Fucking morons. C'mon people— this guy's a con artist. Use your brain. He won't follow through on these promises to you. All he's ever done is screw people over. Don't be duped." He took another large swig from the bottle.

"Damn good thing this guy's got a snowball's chance in hell of making it through the next few primaries, Whitey. But if he ever did get elected, God help us all."

If you enjoyed this book, please leave a brief review at your favorite book site. Thanks!

Sign up for the newsletter at billydecarlo.com to stay informed about progress and release dates for new books, audiobooks, and other news.

Other books by Billy DeCarlo

Billy DeCarlo

Billy DeCarlo is an American author of novels and short stories.

A Note to My Readers

At my core, I'm just a humble, blue-collar guy who has always loved to write. To be honest, I don't seek fame; perhaps just enough fortune to pay the bills. I write because I need to write.

The most rewarding thing a writer can receive is a review from those who enjoyed the work.

The most constructive thing a writer can receive is a private message with anything that can help to improve his or her work.

I do hope that you sign up for the newsletter at my website so that you hear about future books, editions, and other news.

Reviews are the currency of the craft. If you enjoyed my book, please take time to write a review. Thank you and I hope you enjoyed this book!

billydecarlo.com

facebook.com/BillyDeCarloAuthor

twitter.com/BillyDeCarlo1

patreon.com/billydecarlo

goodreads.com/author/show/16887417.Billy_DeCarlo

https://www.amazon.com/Billy-DeCarlo/e/B06XJZF8Z3

Made in the USA
Middletown, DE
28 June 2022

67972571R00177